JUST ONE CHANCE

"Don't budge, either of you. One move . . . just one . . . and you'll go to hell."

Jem Garrett's eyes were bulging. But Colton didn't lose his head. He saw in a flash that during the deputy's progress across the corral would be their only chance to escape, or to down him. At the first shot, the corralled horses would charge around the lawman's area in terror. But if Dylan got clear of the corral and into the yard, he'd have them both.

With a short, falsetto yelp, Rue Colton gave Jem Garrett a shove and leaped toward his horse. The mount shied at the hurtling figure, and Colton fell flat. Jem roared his anger at Colton, ran wildly toward the saloon owner's trotting horse, caught the animal, and threw himself at the saddle just as the darkness flew apart and Rue Colton, on one knee, fired frantically at the shadow in the corral.

Boyd Dylan cursed and ran forward. . . .

Other *Leisure* books by Lauran Paine:
THE RUNNING IRON
TEARS OF THE HEART
LOCKWOOD
THE KILLER GUN
CACHE CAÑON
THE WHITE BIRD
DAKOTA DEATHTRAP

The Dark Trail

LAURAN PAINE

LEISURE BOOKS 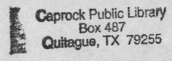 NEW YORK CITY

A LEISURE BOOK®

October 2002

Published by special arrangement with Golden West Literary Agency.

Dorchester Publishing Co., Inc.
276 Fifth Avenue
New York, NY   10001

ISBN: 0-8439-5118-4

Visit us on the web at www.dorchesterpub.com.

Table of Contents

Lawman

I

"Well, that's what a Westerner is, Boyd. I don't give a damn what you've read. Two-gun men or ten-gun men, it's all tripe. You ever smell the sweat on an eager stud horse or the spoor of a horsing mare? Well, don't let it shock you, boy, but that's the best way I can sum it up. Westerners got ideals, but they're damned basic ones. Remember that and you'll get by."

Boyd Dylan nodded shortly, eying Boss Rensberg closely. The sheriff was not a big man, or burly, but an old gun on his shell belt spoke volumes, and the look in his frank blue eyes meant he'd give no lip nor take any. Dylan shrugged, spat into his glove, and snuffed out his cigarette. "Maybe I was wrong, then, Boss. Maybe. . . ."

"Like I told you, Boyd, people are simple out here and their instincts are pretty primitive. Limit most of the trouble in the West to three things and you'll have everything a lawman's got to have. Women, horses, and cattle."

"In that order?"

"Yep. In that order."

Boyd shrugged again. "All right. You know . . . I don't. It just seemed to me that this lady, this Missus Garrett, had as much right to tie her rig in front of Colton's saloon as anybody else, that's all."

"Sure," Boss Rensberg said gently.

"I know how you felt. It's just that her husband and Rue Colton are on the outs over some blotch-branded cattle. Rue sent his boys out to the street to run her off, for that reason,

9

but he used a good excuse. Buggies can't tie to hitch rails. They got to be parallel to the plank walk." Sheriff Rensberg shrugged wearily and looked at his new deputy. "I'll grant you it's kid stuff, running off a woman, but don't take up everything you see in Santa María. It's not wise, or necessary."

"All right, Boss."

The sheriff got to his feet and smiled. He admired Boyd Dylan's powerful shoulders and thick chest. Even the cocky way the young lawman wore his black Stetson, tilted challengingly on the back of his head. But Dylan was new to Oklahoma. Boss didn't want to see him killed over something as foolish as Rue Colton's ancient feud with Jem Garrett.

"I got a little job for you, Boyd." Boss scratched the far side of his drooping, predatory old nose. "Ride out to Powell Plover's place . . . the P Up-And-Down . . . and see if you can make sense out of some complaint he's got about knife-cut cows."

"About what?" Boyd asked.

"Well. . . ." Boss was on the defensive right away. It sounded crazy to him, too. "All I know is what he sent word in about. Said he's got some damned cows that's been slashed with knives."

"That's a new one, Boss. Where is this P Up-And-Down, anyway?"

"Ride north on the stage road four miles, take the left-hand fork, and you'll see the gate with the brand burnt into the crossbar."

Boyd Dylan nodded and went out into the arid, furnace-dry afternoon breeze. His chestnut horse nickered when he went around the hitch rail and ran a finger under the cinch. Dylan, knowing this horse like a book, said nothing, just untied him and walked down past Colton's saloon across the road, and stopped at the water trough. The chestnut dropped his muzzle gratefully, and Dylan stood hip-shot, making a flake-dry cigarette. He was still relaxed and smoking when a tall man on the duckboards under Colton's overhang spoke to him.

"Deputy, you got a lot to learn about Santa María." The voice was not antagonistic. It wasn't friendly, either, just dry, like old cornhusks in the wind.

Dylan looked up, took in the two guns, the bloodless mouth, and the opaque, wide, wild eyes. He didn't answer but just went on smoking, waiting for the chestnut to finish.

"A lot to learn," the man repeated. "And maybe not much damned time to learn it in." This time the voice was decidedly nasty.

Boyd Dylan's face turned upward again. He raked the tall, gaunt gunman with a cold, hostile look. "You got a teacher in mind, feller?"

"Might have. You want a lesson?"

Dylan dropped the reins beside the trough and stepped around the trough, took three steps, and was close to the tall man. He was deliberately close. The gunman would have to use his hands or take a step backward to use his guns. Boyd knew he wouldn't step back. There were too many idlers watching them from the benches along the store fronts under the overhangs.

He nodded. "All right, mister. How about the first lesson?"

The gunman flushed, and the wild eyes flashed down at Dylan. "Sure. Anything to oblige. Next time keep your damned nose out of Rue Colton's business."

"Are you Colton?"

"No, but I'm his. . . ."

It ended there, abruptly and incoherently. Boyd Dylan's fist came up overhand and exploded in the gaunt man's chest,

11

knocking him backward, flailing for balance. Dylan didn't wait. It wasn't his nature, or frontier policy, either. He went in with the ferocity of a maddened Comanche. The gunman tried to cover up under the vicious sledging, tasted the salt of his own blood, staggered, and took two thunderous smashes into the chest that felled him half on, half off the duckboards, face in the pungent moisture where a horse had stood.

Dylan went to his chestnut, fingered the cinch again without being conscious of it, swung up, and rode northward out of Santa María without a backward glance.

Finding the P Up-And-Down was no chore, even for a disgruntled deputy sheriff with anger inside him like a small hot flame. The rancher, Powell Plover, met him before the unpainted old house under the giant sycamores with a friendly nod.

"You come out about them cows?"

Dylan swung down and looped the reins through a handy stud ring in the tree trunk. "Yeah. Boss said something about knife-cut cows."

Plover was a balding man with kindly features and happy eyes. He was the type who went fishing when his troubles began to annoy him.

"Come on," he said. "They're over here in the corral. Damnedest thing I ever heard of. I've seen worked-over brands, docked ear marks, and altered wattles and dewlaps, but I'll be go-to-hell if I ever saw anything like this before, and that's a fact."

Dylan leaned on the corral and looked through the gray old poles. It was a bewildering spectacle to him, too. A swollen, clotted incision was low on the left side of each cow. A lot of pine tar slathered over each animal made the actual slashes look far worse than they were. He shook his head slowly, exasperatedly.

"Damned if I know, Mister Plover. It couldn't be anything but a knife, I reckon. No weed or fence or rock splinter." Dylan turned to face the rancher. "What do you think it is?"

Plover pursed his lips thoughtfully. "Well . . . hell, I got an idea, but it's crazy. Plumb crazy, and that's a fact."

Dylan looked wryly at the cows again. "Nothing could be crazier than knife-cutting a dozen Hereford cows in the guts."

"Well . . . no," Plover conceded. "Just the same I feel sort of foolish, thinking this."

"All right. I know how you feel, but hell, I'm lost in this mess."

"Listen," Plover said suddenly. "A lot of men've died for talking when they shouldn't have. All right. I'm just going to ask you one thing. Give me your word you won't breathe anything I tell you to another soul, then I'll tell you what I think."

"Even Boss Rensberg?" Dylan asked, scowling.

"Even the sheriff. Nobody, damn it."

"All right, Plover, but you're making it damned hard to help you."

"Help me, hell!" Plover exploded. "I don't want any help. I should've kept my mouth shut. I thought that right after I'd sent you word. Well, I done a dumb thing in letting the law know and can't very well undo it, so I'm in the middle." Plover nodded abruptly, still looking at the deputy. "I got your word. Remember that."

"I will."

"Well . . ."—Plover was uncomfortable and showed it—"I found some of Jem Garrett's cows cut up like this last winter and drove 'em home to him. Jem acted annoyed because I'd found 'em. It struck me funny. Shucks, a man'd naturally be indignant if somebody knife-slashed good cows like this, wouldn't he?"

Boyd Dylan nodded, listening.

"Jem wasn't sore, but I got the idea he didn't like me finding the critters and driving 'em home."

"What did you do about it?" Dylan asked.

"Nothing. Not a damned thing. Listen! I mind my own business and ride my own horses and brand my own calves. If Jem had something going on, it didn't concern me. I've never told a soul until this minute."

Boyd Dylan turned slowly and studied the cows again. The cuts seemed to be fleshed under the hide, making a sort of small, swollen pouch. He shook his head in bewilderment, and, when he spoke, it was more to himself than to Powell Plover. "Well, hell, I don't know what to make of it. Critters weren't stabbed deep enough to kill 'em, yet they were cut." He looked at Plover. "Any ideas why it was done?"

Plover shook his head. "Nope. I've figured until I'm blue in the face. It don't make any kind of sense to me."

Dylan turned back toward his horse. The rancher followed him, apparently relieved to see the deputy leaving.

"All right, Plover," the deputy said, "you called me out here, tied my hands, and hobbled me so's I can't do anything." He swung into saddle and looked down at the shorter man. "But I'll be damned if you can stop me from wondering about a few things."

"Like what?" Plover asked.

Dylan reined his horse around and spoke as he rode away, tipping his hat to the cowman. "Why Jem Garrett didn't care about his cows being slashed, and you did. Also, why in the devil it was done in the first place, and finally just what exactly was smuggled into Oklahoma from across the Texas line that runs through your range in those hide pouches cut into your critters."

Powell Plover was too dumbfounded to speak. He

14

watched Dylan ride back toward the stage road with a pop-eyed expression, then turned and hustled back toward the corralled cows with a new interest showing in his features.

II

Boyd Dylan, swinging along slowly, had almost reached the stage road leading to Santa María when a dusty top-buggy hove into sight. It slowed and stopped, awaiting him. He studied it closely as he rode toward it, and got a shock. The driver was the young woman—no more than a girl, she was—whom he had saved from humiliation at Rue Colton's hands that very morning. Susan Garrett. That's what Boss Rensberg had said her name was.

He reined up beside the buggy and looked down into her expressive, beautiful face, admiring her dress and the wholesome maturity of her body in it, as he doffed his hat.

"Ma'am," he said matter-of-factly.

She looked at him quickly. "Deputy Dylan!" she exclaimed, and hurried on before he could speak again. "I'm awfully sorry I caused you trouble this morning. I wouldn't have done it for the world, honestly. I had no idea anyone would object to where I left my buggy. My husband had told me to be sure and tie up at Colton's rail, so I did." She dropped her shoulders in a gesture of resignation. "And what a riot *that* started!"

Her blue eyes would have melted a stone. Boyd Dylan's heart was not stone. It melted that much faster, but not before it fluttered oddly and painfully a few times as he looked at her. She was absolutely breathtaking.

"Please," she murmured, "I'm terrible sorry."

Dylan smiled. It transformed his otherwise hard, severe

face into a wonderfully boyish one.

"Ma'am," he said, "you've got no need to be sorry, or to thank me, either. I'd've done what I did for anybody being embarrassed like you was. My duty, ma'am. But because it *was* you, that just made me do it that much faster." He thought of something suddenly that knocked the flattery and banter out of him. "Your husband *told* you to tie up there in front of Colton's?"

"Yes. That's exactly what he told me to do. In almost those same words, too."

Dylan was looking at her without altogether seeing her. Jem Garrett and Rue Colton were at gun points—everybody said—yet Garrett had deliberately told his wife to tie up where Colton's gunmen were certain to insult her. With that to think about, and the strangeness of Garrett's cows being slashed last winter, and now Plover's cattle, Dylan shook his head.

Sue Garrett's pretty nose wrinkled. "What's wrong?"

"Nothing, ma'am." Boyd Dylan came back to the present. "Tell me something, will you?"

"Certainly. What?"

"What are your husband and Colton at loggerheads about?"

"Cattle. Rue bought some Mexican steers to resell to the Indian agency at Dull Knife. They were turned loose on the range north of town that Jem and a man named Plover, our closest neighbor, use exclusively. The steers had no right to be there, but Rue left them there until he could get drivers to take them to the agency. There was a mix-up when they rounded up. Rue said Jem had kept some of the cattle, and Jem said they were ours. The brands were similar and in the same place and pretty badly burned over. There's been bad blood ever since."

Dylan nodded slowly. It was an old story on the ranges and often enough had ended with more blood spilled than a hatful. He irrelevantly noticed the small beads of perspiration on Sue Garrett's upper lip as he spoke. "Too bad. When did this happen?"

"Last winter."

It clicked into place without actually any basis at all. Plover had discovered slashed cows belonging to Garrett, and Rue Colton's critters had got mixed in with Garrett's. It had all happened last winter. Boyd reached up, scratched his nose idly, looking at the beautiful woman in the buggy, and wondering.

Sue Garrett smiled at him. It was a devastating smile where Dylan's reserve was concerned.

"Well, thank you again, Mister Dylan," she said, "but I'm awfully sorry it happened."

He smiled and nodded, saying nothing. As she drove away, he still just sat there in the blazing sun, watching the buggy whip up dust devils as it jounced along the ruts toward Garrett's JG Slash outfit.

When the buggy was out of sight he faced front in the saddle again, and let his horse amble along in the heat haze. His head was dropped low as he swung toward Santa María. The things he'd seen, heard, and done this morning annoyed him. There was a key somewhere, but it eluded him. Why had Garrett sent his beautiful wife where she would be deliberately insulted and humiliated by his arch-enemy? Why had Garrett been annoyed when Plover had tried to help him with the knife-slashed cattle? What was being smuggled under the animals' hides, and just how much of Plover's yarn was the truth?

Questions were still buzzing in his mind when he swung off his horse before the sheriff's office in Santa María and entered to make his report. But also he meant to have answers to his puzzlers from the sheriff.

Boss Rensberg slouched far down in his chair, idly eying his imported deputy. Boyd Dylan's questions were not consistent, but Boss was no fool, either. He couldn't have been. Not and live as long as he had.

"Well, yes," he finally admitted slowly. "Once, when I was a deputy, there was a lot of smuggling hereabouts. Of course, in them days it was mostly guns and what-not, like powder and ball." Boss shrugged, looking past Dylan's casual, drowsy-looking features, there in the coolness of the office. "Sometimes Mexicans would slip liquor or some other damned thing like stolen jewelry and gold out of Texas, but that stuff wasn't really contraband. Not then. If a man slipped stuff in and out of Mexico, nobody gave a hang. Horses and cattle were different, of course, if they were going *to* Mexico." Boss grinned. His voice was dry and humorous. "*They* got stopped, but to steal them down south and deliver 'em here"—he shrugged—"well, that was all right. The frontier always needed good stock. Besides, we looked on Mexico a little different, then."

"Yeah," Dylan said. "I reckon those days are gone. No more smuggling to worry about now."

"No," the sheriff agreed. "Just the three things I told you about. Women, horses, and cattle."

Dylan got up, stretched, and yawned to hide his crooked, sardonic smile. As he headed for the door, Rensberg watched him curiously.

"Say," the sheriff said abruptly, "what was the matter with Plover? You never did say. Got off on all them damned questions. . . ."

"Oh, he's got a few old cows that look like maybe they've been driven through some barbed wire."

Boss nodded and slapped at the tickling sweat that was cruising the stringy folds of his old neck. "I expected something like that."

Boyd Dylan walked out into the coolness of afternoon shadows and along the duckboards toward the blacksmith shop. He was in front of the sooty old doorway, wide and cool-looking, when a massive, bull-necked man stepped out to bar his way.

"Your name Boyd Dylan?"

The deputy nodded, feeling caution come up out of nowhere, inside of him. "Yes."

"I'm Jem Garrett." The man seemed to be considering what to say next, then decided. "Listen, Dylan, I expect I ought to thank you for helping my wife out today. Well, I do. And I'm going to pass along something else, to sort of even up the obligation. Get to hell out of Santa María. You bare-knuckled Slim Espada this morning. He's going to kill you for that."

Dylan heard the obvious anticipation in Garrett's voice and wondered how a girl as wonderful as Sue Garrett could ever have married a man like this. He nodded thoughtfully, returning the big man's unfriendliness without any effort at all. "Thanks. I appreciate your warning. So his name's Espada. Good. I'll know who to look for, then."

He started forward, directly toward the hulk of a man before him. There was just one thing for Jem Garrett to do, and he did it.

He got out of the way.

Dylan knew the rancher's glare was following him as he walked on down the street, but he didn't care. Resentment and anger he'd thought he had put behind him was bubbling again. Abruptly he altered his course, swung through the manure-stained old roadway, hearing the disturbed buzzing of thousands of flies, crossed the street to the other side of the road, and entered Rue Colton's saloon.

Trade was as listless as the shiny faces and sweat-soaked shirts of the few customers. Dylan spotted his man immediately and walked over to him without hesitation. Slim Espada turned slowly from the bar, watching the deputy approach. Suddenly the lawman stopped short.

He barked: "Espada! You've got until sundown to be out of Santa María. That's an order!"

The two-gun man stared, speechless and amazed. Then he dropped both hands. The two men were not far apart—not more than six feet. The droopy bystanders were galvanized into movement, for at such lethal range neither man could miss. Still, they both held their ground, for you never could tell. Even the annoyed bartender, eyes furious over the interruption to an otherwise dull, complacent day, glared. But he said nothing.

The man who finally spoke into the silence was a medium-sized individual, swarthy and soft-looking. His black eyes were incredulous, for this man, Rue Colton, was more than powerful in Santa María. He *was* the power here.

"Easy, lawman," he said in a modulated tone. "Don't make any mistakes. Are them Boss Rensberg's orders . . . or yours?"

"Mine," Boyd Dylan said. "And they'll stick." He was still looking at Espada. "Sundown, *hombre*, then I'll be hunting you."

No one made a movement or a sound when Dylan left the saloon. No one ever before had bucked the Colton combine, either, and the news traveled like summer fire in the grasslands through Santa María and the country roundabout.

Sue Garrett heard it from Jem when he came home to get a fresh horse and went straight back to town. She felt sick inside, frightened and indignant, too. That deputy sheriff was not only a lion, he was also a jackass. She saddled a horse and rode for Santa María herself. There was no plan in her mind except an insistent desire to tell a man what a complete idiot he was.

Boss Rensberg heard of Boyd's order to Colton's gunman with astonishment, then anger. He suffered Colton to operate, so long as no depredations were committed in his jurisdiction, but that was all. He belonged to an old school. Don't run from trouble, but certainly don't look for it, either. He refilled his shell belt loops and went out looking for Boyd Dylan, but without success.

While Santa María buzzed with wild speculation, the deputy had ridden back to Powell Plover's P Up-And-Down Ranch. The rancher's genial blue eyes welcomed him, if the man's lips didn't. Plover waited for the deputy to dismount, but Dylan didn't. From his horse's back he talked to the rancher.

"Listen, Plover, I want you to do something."

"Now, wait a minute. I told you this morning. . . ."

"What makes you think it's got to do with those cows, or trouble?" Boyd asked mildly.

"Well," Plover shot right back with a head-wagging grin, "I know your kind, lawman. I've seen 'em before. By hell, you could be sitting quietly in church, and trouble'd hunt you and just naturally blow up around you. No, dammit all! Like I said before, I mind my own business. I'm a cowman, not a gunfighter."

"All right. You don't have to be a gunman to do what I'm going to ask you to do."

"Well? What is it?"

Dylan grinned in spite of himself. Plover was so irate, his discomfort so militant. The deputy almost bowled the man

21

over when he said: "Ride over to Garrett's and ask Sue Garrett to ride back here with you."

"What?"

"No, it's not what you're thinking, either. She *is* beautiful, though, isn't she? I just want her to tell me a couple of things I don't dare ask her around Jem."

"Not by a gut I won't," Plover said flatly, vehemently. "No, sir!" His voice changed then, became gentle, explanatory, a tone such as he would use when expostulating with recalcitrant little boys. "Listen, lawman, you're going to stir up a hornet's nest around here. Sue's holding every damned heart in the Santa María country right in her hands, just like Jem's got everybody disliking and fearing him more than they do even that string-bean Mex gunman of Rue's. For hell's sake be careful! What happens to you is your own affair, but you let one word slip out about what I told you this morning, and Rue'll be after me in a second." Plover groaned. "He'll know damned well where it came from, too, even if not a word is said about me. Rue's no fool. Not by a damned sight, and that's a fact."

"Well . . . all right, then," Dylan said. "Tell me something. Is Jem Garrett pretty well fixed?"

"I don't know." Plover's eyes wavered a little. "But he don't owe nobody, and he's always got money and good horses."

Dylan nodded. "Thanks. You'd better ride into town this afternoon. There's going to be fireworks."

"Fireworks? What kind?"

The deputy said matter-of-factly: "I ordered Slim Espada to be out of Santa María by sundown. I don't think he'll go." He swung his horse around without another word.

Plover watched the deputy sheriff ride out of his yard for the second time the same day. Fright and horror showed on

22

the rancher's face. He was still rooted to the hot, dusty ground when Boyd Dylan rode out of sight, heading for the stage road back to town.

III

Squinting at the rider loping along a short distance ahead of him, Boyd Dylan was aware that something insistent in his memory was nagging at him. He lifted his horse into an ambling gallop and followed the rider until he was close enough to recognize the lithe figure of Sue Garrett. When he overtook her, she swung around with surprise and consternation on her lovely face.

"Carrying the mail, ma'am?" He grinned.

Sue looked at him and reined up her horse, but said nothing for a while. Then abruptly she urged her mount through the brush toward three mighty cottonwoods at the right of the trail. Beneath them, she stopped her horse, looking back at Dylan. He followed her in silence.

"You're going to be killed, Mister Deputy," she announced as he drew up alongside her, and into it she put all the calm irony she could, looking at Boyd Dylan levelly. "What's the matter with you? Wasn't bearding Colton's gunman this morning enough? Do you *have* to go deliberately out of your way to get killed?"

He was more interested in the curves of her lush body, silhouetted against the brassy sky, and in admiring the proud challenge of her jutting breasts, the compact firmness of her. He swung down beside her horse, loosening the cinch of his own mount for something to do with his hands. He couldn't look at her as he spoke.

"Ma'am," he said earnestly, "I've got an idea Santa

María'd be better off without the Espada *hombre*. Without Colton, too, for that matter."

Sue's shock was reflected in the stilted way in which she spoke.

"Oh, you fool! That gunman, Espada, is bad enough. He'll kill you. But Rue Colton! Why, he's wealthy and influential. Not powerful just in Santa María, either, but in the whole territory!" She was shaking her head in an aggrieved way as he came around his horse toward her.

He held up a hand to help her dismount. The shade under the cottonwoods would be wonderful, after coming out of the blistering heat. She leaned forward and took his hand to dismount. An electric shock passed through Dylan, and an almost irrepressible urge to close his fist over the small fingers and hold on.

"Missus Garrett"—he spoke with sour gravity, thinking of her massive, hulking husband and his unsavoriness—"I just asked a man to ride to your ranch and fetch you to me."

She glanced up at him in surprise. Hot color mounted to her cheeks.

"I want to ask you some questions," he said.

"This man you asked . . . Powell Plover, wasn't it?" she asked hesitantly.

"What makes you think that?"

Sue shrugged. "Oh, nothing. I just knew, that's all."

"Is Plover a friend of yours?"

"I like Powell. Jem doesn't. Not since last winter."

Boyd Dylan almost told her why, for somehow he felt certain she had no inkling of the reason for her husband's dislike of Plover. Almost he told her about how Plover had nosed in with the cut cows. But he didn't. He just nodded gently, wondering at himself, at the effect that the loveliness of this woman—another man's wife—was having on his heart.

24

"Well," he said, "it don't make any difference who he was, anyway, because he refused to go."

"That wouldn't surprise me."

"Why?"

Sue's eyes were bitter. "Men in the Santa María country don't cross Jem Garrett."

"Not even Colton?"

She shrugged. "I don't know. Why do you ask?"

"You're beautiful," Dylan said, and he said it mechanically, as he would state his age. Sue, too startled to speak, just looked at him dumbfounded. But he didn't meet her eyes as he went on: "I'm asking for two reasons, ma'am. In the first place, I don't believe your husband and Rue Colton are enemies at all. In the second place, I believe both Colton and your Jem are outlaws."

Sue's face paled, and her eyes were suddenly terrified. Still she said nothing, regarding the deputy without blinking, standing erect and motionless.

"That's why I wanted to talk to you," Dylan said. "To say nothing of the pleasure it gives me just to look at you." She opened her lips to speak then, but his curt slash of the air with one hand stopped her. "Does Jem have enough income from his cattle to live and spend the way he does?"

Sue was shaken. "I . . . don't know what you mean."

"Yes, you do. Listen, Sue Garrett. There's trouble ahead. Real trouble. Is that why you were riding to town?"

"Yes, but not for the reason you think. Not to warn Jem. He already knew. He's the one who told me there was trouble afoot, when he came home and changed horses."

"They why were you going?"

"Because. . . ." It seemed almost to strangle her to say it. It had seemed so right to her before, but after what he'd said, it didn't seem proper, her real reason for going to town.

"Because?" Dylan prompted.

"Because I wanted to warn you. I owe you that much"—she spoke defensively—"after this morning."

"No, you don't owe me a thing. I told you I'd've done as much for anybody."

"Well, that's why I was going to town."

"I appreciate that, Sue. Now answer my question."

"About Jem?"

"Yes."

"He runs cattle. That's all I know."

"Is it? Well, what do you suspect, then?"

Her eyes were flying danger flags now. "Jem is my husband! I won't. . . ."

"That," Dylan interrupted solemnly, "is the worst news I've ever heard in my whole damned life . . . ma'am."

"Stop it! Please go away! Leave us . . . leave Santa María alone. Forget Jem and Rue and the rest. Let old Boss Rensberg run things the way they've always been run."

"You mean," the deputy asked ironically, "like they were run thirty, forty years ago? Sort of slipshod and easy-like?" He shook his head. "I can't, Sue. I just don't see things like that. Not in that light."

She stared fixedly into his face, then spun quickly back to her horse, and fisted the reins. Boyd Dylan's hand closed around her shoulders and spun her to face him. Then, scarcely knowing what he was doing, he pulled her to him. She gave a shocked, startled cry and swung an open hand at his face. He ducked it automatically and pulled her closer—and the next moment, to his complete amazement, their lips were locked together in a kiss that he vaguely felt must somehow be unending.

"Good . . . Lord!" A small, frightened voice said that. Sue's.

Dylan said nothing. For a moment more he still held her, but at arm's length, too astonished to say a word of any kind. Then he let his arms drop.

"Men live and die in no more time than that, Sue," he said. "So falling in love in less than ten seconds doesn't seem so impossible, does it?"

She didn't answer. He could see again the stricken look in her eyes he had seen before.

"Why did you do that?" she asked almost inaudibly.

Boyd Dylan's boyish smile flashed. It was such a ridiculous question. He thought of her angry strike at him.

"In self-defense," he murmured.

Both laughed then, not altogether happily, but in relief, anyway.

The first long shadows were warning of the coming close of day when, at Sue's insistence, Dylan mounted and rode on toward Santa María, leaving her there. He had to agree with her that it would be anything but an intelligent move for them to be seen riding even the open road together.

Evening was fast approaching when he rode into town. Santa María at sundown was an unreal clutch of blistered, dusty old buildings, trying to look prosperous and decent under the benevolent light of the failing sun. It almost succeeded, at that, for the harsh corners were softened in shadow, and the smell of curling grass and parched earth cooling gave off their distinctive perfumes.

Boyd Dylan rode into town from the south end, reversing his usual procedure. Nor did he, as usual, stable his horse at the livery barn. He tied up in a side street—alley would fit better—and started off down through Santa María in a slow walk.

He was attuned to what he knew was happening and what

had happened. Santa María was as silent as a tomb. Even the piano in Colton's place was without its usual challengers. Boyd sensed hundreds of eyes following him. He knew, too, that Espada had word, by now, of his arrival.

He thought of many things fleetingly, but always came back to Sue and what she had said, after that kiss, before he had left her and ridden on into town to keep rendezvous with a killer. Always, just behind his memory of Sue's beauty, was the threatening shadow of her husband's hard face. Dylan's resentment grew steadily.

It was still growing when Boss Rensberg walked out of his office, across the road, and hailed his deputy.

"Hey . . . Boyd! Come over here. Listen! Cut that out."

Boyd didn't look around. He knew the kind of men he was up against. Espada and Colton. Either would as soon ambush a man as eat. One slight error in vigil and Boyd Dylan would be a dead man.

But the sheriff persisted angrily, starting across the road toward his deputy, kicking up spirals of dust that furred his shapeless old pant legs.

"Boyd! I'm warning you! You made a fool play, boy. You got no right to be giving orders like that."

Dylan stopped in his tracks, only faintly conscious of Rensberg's garrulous ramblings. Slim Espada had just sauntered out of Rue Colton's place. Boss saw him, too, at the same instant, and checked both his progress and his words.

The tension was almost insufferable. Espada studied the deputy scornfully, walking casually toward the center of the road. They were about a hundred feet apart when he stopped, faced Dylan squarely, and spoke.

"All right, lawman. It's sundown, and I'm still here. Your move."

Dylan's eyes were wide. He made no move to face the gunman from the center of the road.

"You can still slope, *hombre!*" he called.

Espada laughed dryly, a sound like snails dropping off a wet wall and cracking their fragile shells when they landed. "No, I'm not running, lawman. Not the running kind." His head inclined in just a bare minimum of a nod. "You gave the order. You back it up."

Dylan studied the man's thin, terra-cotta-colored hands and braced himself. It would come any second now—and fast. Blindingly fast. For this one single moment the initiative was his—and he took it!

IV

The thunder of gunfire blew the silence apart. The echoes chased each other down the land. Of the two men, Espada was a shade faster, but, oddly, his first shot had been ten inches wide of his mark. It was one of those things that happen freakishly to the best of gunmen, but in this case it was a fatal blunder.

Dylan felt the tug of Espada's next bullet. He was standing sideward, and it plowed burningly across his rounded right shoulder. He, too, fired a second time, and that slug also took effect. Espada went down reluctantly, his head hanging forward on his chest.

Boss Rensberg walked up slowly, silent and thin-lipped. He passed Dylan with scarcely a glance. The deputy was still standing, and that was enough for the sheriff. Boss stood wide-legged, staring at Slim Espada, then he bent over, took both guns from the lifeless fingers, straightened with an effort, and looked around.

The duckboards were filling again with curious townsmen

and riders from the range country. Boss turned his back on the dead man and walked back to Dylan. He saw the telltale scarlet high on the deputy's right shoulder as he came up.

"Bad?" he asked grimly.

Dylan shook his head. "No, I hardly feel it at all. Just a mile high to do much real damage. Is he dead?"

"Dead as he can get." Boss looked down at the big guns in his hands. "Here. You won 'em."

Boyd looked at the guns distastefully. "I don't collect scalps. Keep 'em."

"Well . . . all right. But listen, Boyd, you had no right to order him out of town, y'know."

Boyd looked boldly at the older law officer. "Boss," he said, "I don't know how to say it. Maybe things're different now from what they were when you first went into the law business. There's no way to overlook or compromise with outlaws any more. You fight 'em any old way they want it, and break 'em." A sardonic expression wreathed Boyd Dylan's face. "Oh, I know I've got no business telling you how to law. I expect the best thing for me to do is resign and ride on." Rensberg had made no attempt to speak before, and now, as he got his mouth open, Dylan cut him off. "All right. I'll do that, but first I want to talk to Jem Garrett and Rue Colton."

He turned and strode back toward his horse. The silent watchers along his route stepped hastily aside, nodding respectfully as he went down the plank walk. His ringing spurs could have been a knell for the man he had just killed.

Jem Garrett and Rue Colton were still leaning against the wall on either side of the saloon's solitary front window. It had all happened so abruptly, so devastatingly, they were still stunned.

Colton turned his head and fisted his hands deep in his

pants pockets, staring at nothing. "Damn! I still don't believe it."

Jem Garrett, more realistic and cynical, grunted. "Something went wrong. I seen Slim draw. It was like always, only this time his right-hand gun seemed to snag as the barrel was coming up." He shook his shaggy head. "Too bad."

There was nothing but lip service in the words, but they brought Rue Colton's mind out of his shock.

"Jem, that deputy's got to be killed! Before this, I thought he was just another blow-hard lawman. Now I figure different. He's dangerous!"

"Well," Garrett said dryly, "I'm sure not in his class. Not when he came that close to outgunning Slim."

Colton's black eyes pin-pointed Garrett. "Listen, Jem, I can't hire another gunman fast enough to put him away before he smells something out. You'll *have* to do him in. There's a bonus of five hundred for him dead, Jem. Do it any way you want, but do it."

Garrett grunted again, looking at Colton wryly. "I'll see if I can dry-gulch him tonight, but, dammit, don't think I'm going up against him out in the open."

"I don't care *how* you do it. Just do it!" The color returned to Colton's face. "Now you'd better slope. We've been too careful about building up this enmity between us, for Santa María's benefit, to be seen together."

Garrett nodded. "How about the divvy?"

Colton shook his head. "Not here. I just finished with it this morning, anyway. I'll ride out to your barn tonight, same time as always, and give you your share. You sure Plover don't suspect anything?"

"Naw. He's too dumb. Last winter he run into some cows of mine we used, like I told you then, and he didn't suspect nothing. I knew he didn't, because if he had, the word

31

would've got around."

Colton nodded. "Just the same, next time you pick the critters, do it in the daytime so's you don't make that mistake of getting any of his again."

Jem Garrett didn't answer. It rankled, to be reminded of having made an error. He turned toward the rear of the saloon and walked away. Colton watched him thoughtfully, and shrugged.

Boyd Dylan's shoulder ached a little, but the bullet groove wasn't deep. He got it dressed by the local doctor, then went to Colton's place and had a drink. In the thick silence that settled over the saloon while he was there he was told that Rue Colton wasn't in town—something he suspected was a lie and was—and left.

At the livery barn he got his horse and took it up to the blacksmith shop for new shoes all around. The smith, a squatty, massive man whose tremendous muscles rolled mightily under his sweaty hide looked at the deputy speculatively. He led the horse to a cross-tie and made him fast.

"Halter-puller?" he asked.

"No. He's quiet."

"Yeah, he looks it." The smith bent and lifted the horse's left front hoof, eying the worn shoe critically. He was fishing in a shoeing box for the pullers when his voice rumbled from deep within his brawny chest to ask: "You get hit by that left-hand gun?"

"A nick on top of the shoulder."

"Lucky . . . damned lucky. I've seen him in action before. He's awful fast. Colton'll be lost without him, I'll bet on that."

Dylan fished around in a shirt pocket for his tobacco sack, leaned back, and rolled one, thinking. At last he asked: "This

Colton . . . he's a friend of yours?"

"No. I drink in his saloon and he has his horses shod here, and that's about it. He's too big a man for me to mess with."

"How about Jem Garrett? I bumped into him coming out of here this morning."

"Jem's just another piney-woods cowman to me. I shod his sorrel horse this morning." The smith grunted and straightened up, shooting Boyd a glance and fishing for his knife and hoof-nippers. "He's got the best damned horses in the country, though. Has a regular weakness for fine horse-flesh."

Dylan listened, making no answer. An ironic thought flashed into his mind. Jem Garrett was a judge of more. He was a good judge of flesh, horse and otherwise.

The smith bent to his labors again, sweat glistening on his upper body like a sheen of oil. "Jem's good pay, too," he went on, then hesitated. He straightened up suddenly and fished under his scarred apron. A thick, padded hand came out holding up something bright and thick. "Take a look at that. First triangle I've seen in years. They used to be pretty common around Santa María when I was a kid. There was a lot of gold hereabouts then. It's all gone now. Has been for twenty years or so." The smith's face screwed up confidentially. "You know what I think? I'll lay you odds Jem's got a hidden gold mine on his damned ranch!"

Boyd was electrified. The thing he was holding in his palm was a wedge of hand-smelted gold in conventional frontier triangle pattern. Small as it was, it was worth possibly fifty dollars. A thumbnail gouged it easily. Pure, raw gold.

His heart was pounding when he handed the thing back in silence. The smith pocketed it and bent to his labors once more.

"He might have, at that," Dylan said. "He's always pretty

33

well moneyed, isn't he? I mean, he's got more than enough for a man who runs a few Mexican cows, I'd say."

It was a shot in the dark, and a weak one, but it worked.

The smith nodded. "Yeah, Jem's always ready to spend his money, all right. He don't get that stuff from peddling a few old hides a year. I'll bet on that."

"Yeah," Boyd Dylan agreed vaguely.

It was torture, standing around making small talk until his horse was shod, but he did it. Then he led the animal back to the livery barn, saddled up, and swung north out of town, his insides tight with anticipation.

He knew now what was being smuggled across the line into Oklahoma, in those cruel little pouches slit in the cows' hides. No one would stop a cattle drive looking for contraband. It was a clever way to smuggle gold. The deputy was cynical about it, too. It was far too clever a dodge for a man of Jem Garrett's caliber to think of. It was more the sort of thing Rue Colton would think of.

He thought of Powell Plover's critters and frowned. Somehow, in some way, a mistake had been made. Plover's cattle had been used. Except for that the system might have gone on indefinitely without detection.

He thought of Sue Garrett then, as he rode slowly down the lane toward the P Up-And-Down. It made him writhe inside, too. He was after Jem Garrett and meant to take him. Sue wouldn't admire the man who humbled her husband. Or would she?

He was still wrestling with the problem when he rode into Plover's yard and saw the rancher saddling a horse.

" 'Evening," he greeted.

Plover regarded him stonily. "You done it, didn't you?"

"You mean Espada?"

"Yeah."

"Yes. He had his choice."

There was a brief, awkward silence, then Plover sagged a little, standing at the head of his saddled horse. "You didn't say nothing about me, about the cows, did you?"

"Nope. I told you I wouldn't. Why?"

"Well, I was just getting ready to ride into town and find you."

"What for? Scared?"

Plover's color came up. He nodded vigorously. "You're damned right I am. You're sitting on a powder keg, and I'm right beside you. You're a gunman, I'm a cowman. I couldn't begin to get away from Colton's mob if you was to let it slip I told you about my cows."

"Is that what you were coming after me for?" It didn't figure to Boyd Dylan.

"No," Plover said tartly, jerking a thumb over his shoulder toward the unpainted little house. "Sue's in there. She wants you. I don't."

Dylan blinked owlishly, stunned. "Sue Garrett . . . in there?"

"Yes." Plover looked up at Dylan again. His eyes reflected all the fear and discomfort of a harassed man. "Listen, lawman . . . do me a favor. Take her away from here. Jem'll come a-gunning as sure as God made green apples, and that's a fact. He'll miss her and start out looking. I'm his nearest neighbor. Get her out of here, will you?"

Dylan didn't answer. He swung down, looped the reins over a corral post, and started for the house without another glance at Powell Plover.

V

Plover watched Boyd Dylan walk away and grimaced at the deputy's back. He turned to his own waiting horse, regarded it distastefully, ashamed of the flight he had planned. Looking back toward the house where Dylan had disappeared through the sagging front door, he shrugged resignedly, then led the horse back into the barn and began listlessly to unsaddle him.

When he was hanging his gear back on the wall, the carbine butt caressed his cheek. It was cool and smooth—and reassuring. Plover pulled it from the saddle boot, studied it thoughtfully, then went over to the shadow of the barn door and sat down on a nail keg. As he looked out into the failing light of day, over toward Jem Garrett's JG Slash, he cradled the little rifle over his knees and stroked it uneasily.

At that same moment, inside his ranch house, Boyd Dylan was calling anxiously: "Sue?" Boyd saw her in the shadows. He knew, then, from the way she came toward him that the kiss had meant as much to her as it had to him. "What are you doing over here at Plover's?" he asked her.

"I couldn't go back home," she said pleadingly. "I can't explain it to you . . . I can't! But I just couldn't go."

He reached for her, and she came to him willingly enough. "Sue," he whispered, "I love you! Is that impossible? I mean I shouldn't, should I, because you're married?"

"I wanted you to love me, lawman. I've wanted you to since much earlier. When you stood up for me at Colton's tie rack. It wasn't just the kiss. It was before that. I'm shameless, too."

"Because you're married?"

"Yes, because of that. But . . . I'll go with you. I'll be whatever you want me to be. I can't help it. I love you!"

Boyd Dylan's heart was making rhythmic thunder in his ears. The air in the Plover ranch house seemed stiflingly hot. "No," he said, "I don't want you any way at all. Just as my wife. Will you divorce him?"

"Yes. I've tried to before. Twice. The first time he beat the idea out of me. The second time . . . well, that was today. I made up my mind when he said he was going to kill me if I was home when he got back from watching you get killed. That's why I'm here."

"Waiting, Sue?"

"Waiting and praying. If you hadn't come back within an hour with Powell . . . after I'd sent him to get you . . . I was going to ride on, leave Santa María." Her face was pressed so close to his chest that her voice came to him muted, muffled, but wonderfully understandable." I had one brief memory to take with me . . . your kiss. But it would have been more than enough to have made all the suffering I've known worthwhile. It's a finer treasure than anything in the two years of memories I have of being married to Jem."

He could feel her tightening against him and knew the tears, just below the surface now, would be assuaging to taut, raw nerves. "Well, honey," he murmured, "if anyone rides on now, it'll be both of us." He felt mean about asking the next question that came into his mind then, but he asked it anyway. "Is Rue Colton your husband's pardner in this gold-smuggling business?"

She looked up, reaching for his neck with both arms. "I don't know, darling. Honestly. Jem's awfully secretive. All I know is that he makes a lot of cattle drives. Buys them sometimes in Texas, and brings them home. Other times he drives

37

our cattle to Texas and returns with them or others. He's always been careful not to let me know what he's doing, and I've hated him too much to care."

Dylan relaxed to the pressure of her arms. Their lips came together again, and he breathed in the sweetness of her breath. The kiss lasted until her passionate breathing became ragged, then he pulled back a little, but only to succumb again and meet her moist, silky full lips once more. There was an almost tangible sense of ecstasy stirring within him.

"Sue," he told her then, "I was afraid, before. Even now, I don't exactly know what to tell you. I'm a lawman, honey, and your husband's an outlaw. I've got a job to do. Will you wait for me here, until I get back?"

"Where are you going?"

"To the JG Slash. I want to look at Jem's cows. Sort of nose around."

She looked up at him with the old, stricken, frightened look. "Jem . . . is he still in Santa María?"

Without knowing, or caring, but to allay her fears, Dylan nodded. "I reckon so. Anyway, you stay here. I'll fix it with Plover. When I come back, we'll ride on."

"Yes," she said fervently. "I'll wait right here, Boyd, if it takes a hundred years. I love you so!" The confession was spoken wildly, passionately, but naturally.

He bent and kissed her again. She took one of his sinewy hands and placed it between the fullness of her ripe breasts. He could feel the jolting slams of her heart in irregular cadence, and smiled.

"Me too, darling. *Adiós*."

As Garrett rode due west from the P Up-And-Down toward Garrett's place, the wandering daylight grew mellow with orange shades. The deputy's emotions were a jumble of confusion, but he promised himself one thing. Come what might, he would not be the man to gun down Jem Garrett. The desire to kill the renegade was there, as well as more than enough hatred, fed by the memory of Sue's remark about Jem having beaten her. It was just that, if he killed the man himself, the specter of the dead husband would always be between Sue and Boyd, regardless of whether Sue had loved Jem or not.

Dylan felt old and tired when at last he topped a land swell and began the descent toward ghostly, unpainted buildings nestling in a beautiful little valley below. He recalled Powell Plover's fidgeting when he had asked the route to the JG Slash and grinned. Plover had agreed to stay home until Dylan came back or, if he didn't, to wait until definite word of his death came. Then he would help Sue escape from the Santa María country.

Plover's face had been deathly white in the dying daylight, but he had promised. Dylan thought of him, hunkered in his barn with a carbine over his knees, scared half to death. Dylan was grinning again as he swung down in a clump of scrub oak. He left his horse and spurs behind, and began inching toward the dark, sinister-looking ranch buildings.

The JG Slash seemed deserted. There were four good horses in a corral by the log barn that caught his scent and looked toward him, ears up and heads forward. Boyd went toward them, saw that the manger was empty, and felt better. If they hadn't been fed yet, Jem probably wasn't on the ranch.

He moved off toward the barn, stepped inside, and stood still, letting his eyes become accustomed to the gloom. It was while he was motionless that the sound of cattle came to him faintly. Driven cattle, he could tell, by their protesting sounds. Wondering, he made a fast, cursory examination of the barn's interior and found nothing but some old rags soaked with blood.

The cattle were coming closer. Dylan went outside to make a guess at their route. He didn't want anyone stumbling onto his tied saddle horse, but the mount was safe. The cattle were being driven out of the night west of the barn, toward the network of corrals.

Dylan surmised that Jem Garrett was bringing in another herd to be used in the drive south, into Texas, where the contraband gold would be sewed into their hides before they were driven leisurely back home again. He stayed in the shadows close to the barn, watching. A rider loped up out of the warm night with its Comanche moon and weak, moist light, and opened a corral gate, spun his horse, and rode back out of sight again.

Dylan recognized the big hulk of a man—Jem Garrett. The deputy loosened his gun in its holster, then shoved it down deeper again. He wanted Garrett alive. The gun was useless in the face of his resolve.

Cattle came out of the night like dark silhouettes, moving on legs that propelled them only because they were being pushed. Dylan tried to count them but gave it up when they began streaming through the gate opening, three and four abreast, in a riot of scorching, heavy dust and rattling horns. He didn't move again until the lone rider swung down, kicked the gate closed, and snapped the chain.

He anticipated the man's next move. He sidled toward the barn where Jem Garrett would unsaddle. Boyd Dylan was smiling to himself as he made use of every shadow and cover to get close to the unsuspecting outlaw. It would be almost too easy.

Garrett unsaddled and put the horse in the same corral with the others the deputy had seen. The cattleman dumped his saddle, bridle, and blanket unceremoniously on the ground and went inside, reaching for a pitchfork that hung between two nails just inside the door.

Dylan waited until he saw the fragrant hay being forked out the opening in the side of the barn into the horse's manger, then started to close in, drawing his gun. He was moving around the side of the barn, north of the corrals, when a loping horse coming in from the east stopped him in his tracks.

Listening, Dylan knew the animal was being ridden, was not traveling loose. Hurriedly, frantically, he looked around for cover. The best available hiding place was by the big, slab watering trough in the horse corral. He holstered his gun, slid through the corral stringers, and darted toward it.

He had just barely hunkered down, squeezing his six-foot frame into a lump that blended with the darkness, when the rider loomed into sight and swung down.

VI

Jem Garrett came stamping out of the barn, tossing the pitchfork away as he came, and squinted toward the dismounted rider. Recognition came slowly to Boyd Dylan because he didn't know Rue Colton's outline as well as he might. It was Colton's voice that identified him for the deputy.

"Jem, I got. . . ."

"You bring the divvy, Rue?" Garrett cut in harshly.

"Yes. Here." Two pouches passed between them, then, when Colton spoke again, there was an urgency to his voice that made Jem Garrett look at him quickly. "Listen, Jem. That old gaffer, Rensberg, is up to something."

"What're you talking about?"

"I'm not sure. After this whelp Dylan downed Slim, old Boss came over to the saloon with blood in his eye. First time

41

I ever seen him get that way."

"Get to the point, dammit," Garrett said edgily.

"Boss told me to get rid of my boys and either clean up my business or get out of Santa María."

"He can't talk like that, the damned old goat."

"Well, he did. I don't think he suspects a thing about the gold, but. . . ."

"I'll tell you what's biting him," Jem Garrett cut in. "He thinks that imported deputy of his is all wool and a yard wide. He's sore because of the risk this Dylan's running. Well, damn his lights, he'd better worry, I'm going to kill that. . . ."

"You mean you haven't done it yet? Jem, I told you. . . ."

"What am I supposed to do . . . use Injun magic to bring him where he can be bushwhacked? I haven't seen him since the fight in town. He rode out right after that, remember? And I had things to do."

"Well"—Colton's eyes went to the bawling, milling cattle in the corral—"you'd better turn these cattle back out. We'll just have to slack off for a while. At least until this deputy's done for. By hell, we'd better just down old Boss, too. He's getting his neck up, and I don't like it."

"Are you crazy?" Garrett demanded. "Just who in hell's going to do all these killings? I'm not. You'd better send word down the back trails you need another two-gun man."

"I thought of that, while I was riding out here. We could bring one of those Mex killers out of Texas. One of the gang that're looting the stages for this gold we buy at a dime on the dollar."

Jem Garrett was shaking his head even before Colton finished speaking. "Nope. That end of things is working too smoothly. Don't mess it up by taking a man away and having to break in a new one."

"Well?" Colton said. "What then?"

Garrett was silent for a while. When he spoke, his voice was sullen. "I don't know. We'll just lie low for a while. I'll knock off that troublesome deputy. Old Rensberg'll raise hell and prop it out with a chunk, but in time he'll forget it. Then we can get back to our smuggling again. It's too good to let die."

Rue Colton sighed loudly. The sound carried to where Dylan lay, his cramped legs aching. The deputy had his gun out, ready when Colton spoke again.

"Well, dammit, let's go get some coffee. This thing's got me worried a little."

"Coffee, sure, but no food. I can't cook, and Sue's not here."

"Not here?" Colton echoed in surprise. "You mean she's not home from town, or something?"

"Hell, I don't know. She just ain't here. Wasn't home when I got back from town. Her horse is gone, too. Maybe the damned fool's finally run away, like she said she would." Garrett's big shoulders rose and fell in annoyance. "Good riddance."

Colton licked his lips nervously. "You're through with her, Jem?"

"Hell, yes."

"I'll make you a deal. That big Denton gelding for her. I'll bring the horse out in the morning. You bring her in to the saloon as soon as she comes back."

"All right." Jem Garrett nodded grimly. "That's a trade. But what if she don't come back?"

"Then we'll track her down and bring her back."

Boyd Dylan had heard more than enough. He knew about the gold. Its source and all. Jem Garrett had enough evidence in the two pouches in his pockets right now to convict them both. Just one thread remained. The thieves in Texas who stole the money. But that was a job for the Texas Rangers.

It was the callous trade for Sue that brought Dylan's fighting blood up in a gorge of murderous fury. He stood up suddenly, and cocked his .45. The sound carried. The horses at the manger shied and snorted softly, eying him distrustfully. His voice was low and clear even before Garrett and Colton turned in their tracks to locate him.

"Don't budge, either of you. One move . . . just one . . . and you'll go to hell."

Jem Garrett's eyes were bulging. But Colton didn't lose his head. He saw in a flash that during the deputy's progress across the corral would be their only chance to escape, or to down him. At the first shot, the corralled horses would charge around the lawman's area in terror. But if Dylan got clear of the corral and into the yard, he'd have them both.

With a short, falsetto yelp, Rue Colton gave Jem Garrett a shove and leaped toward his horse. The mount shied at the hurtling figure, and Colton fell flat. Jem roared his anger at Colton, ran wildly toward the saloon owner's trotting horse, caught the animal, and threw himself at the saddle just as the darkness flew apart and Rue Colton, on one knee, fired frantically at the shadow in the corral.

Boyd Dylan cursed and ran forward. By the flash of Colton's shot he saw Garrett escaping, and flung himself over the corral stringers with a curse. Leveling his pistol at the kneeling man, he fired. Colton sagged, straightened, and swung his gun up again. Dylan's second shot knocked him sideward in a sodden heap. Rue Colton's cocked gun lay in the dust beside him.

Dylan was tumbling down from the top pole of the corral when Jem Garrett, twisting in the saddle, snapped off his first shot. It wasn't even close. The deputy took deliberate aim and squeezed the trigger. The horse gave a great lunge forward, then went jolting forward in a rocky gait inspired by terror and the pain of a twisted ankle.

When the horse didn't fall, Boyd holstered his gun, tossed the inert Colton a quick glance, and sprinted for his own mount. Jem Garret had gained precious seconds. Dylan clawed at the tie-rope, swung up, and whirled east again, listening to the faint, uneven hoof beats of the horse the man rode, then roared out in pursuit.

He rode all the way to Santa María and still didn't sight his prey. Bewildered, certain the injured animal would be down by now, he met Boss Rensberg riding out of town.

The sheriff eyed him dourly. "I been thinking," he said without preface. "I got a suspicion when you was asking me about smuggling this morning. Colton's no good, or Jem either, for that matter, and I want to know what's going on. 'Course, they hate each other, so I figure Jem, who used to be pretty friendly with Rue, could tell me about what Rue's up to."

Boyd nodded impatiently. "You seen Jem in town?"

Boss shook his head. "Nope. I looked for him. It would've saved me this darned night ride, if he'd been around. Why?"

"Well, ride along with me. I got a few things to tell you."

Boyd Dylan began to tell them, and he didn't finish speaking until they were turning into the lane to Powell Plover's P Up-And-Down. After the deluge of words stopped, Boss Rensberg rode along, head low on his chest and hands clasped with the reins over his saddle horn.

"I'll be damned," he muttered. "Completely and absolutely damned." He looked over at his deputy. "You was right, Boyd. Things *have* changed since I commenced lawing." He shook himself like a dog coming out of the water and squinted ahead at the dark, sinister-looking outline of the Plover house and barn. "Well, Jem Garrett won't get far,

45

that's a gut. One good thing about telegraph." He shrugged. "All right, son, you done it. Now listen . . . I expect you think I'm an old moss-back. You might be a mite right at that, but I want you to do me a favor."

"What?"

The sheriff grinned. "Well, don't get your nose out of joint because I didn't go along with you in this thing. Stay on being my deputy. I got reason to need new blood around me, Boyd. I got a lot to learn. Things've changed, boy. They sure as hell have." He reined up suddenly and pointed to something dark and lumpy in the foreground. "What's that? If it ain't a man or a horse, I'll kiss your foot."

"Hold it, you two. Right where you are!"

The words came at them with all the vigor and threat that was possible in a man who means what he says. Dylan's heart was in his throat. It was Garrett's horse, and the dead horse meant that Jem Garrett had ridden for Plover's place.

The voice of the hidden man growled at them again. "Who are you?"

The sheriff answered, biting off each word angrily. "Sheriff and deputy sheriff of Santa María County. You come out in the open with that gun, *hombre,* then toss it down!"

To Dylan's amazement, the man came out of the barn, jettisoned the carbine, and strolled over to them. He had never seen an ugly face that looked so good to him.

"Powell! Where's Sue?"

Plover jerked his thumb over his shoulder. "In the barn. She come running out after I shot Jem, there. He come riding in here on a half-dead horse and threatened to kill me if I didn't give him another." Plover's face beamed genially, proudly. "I don't have horses to give away, so I just ups with the carbine and shoots him down." He looked at Boss Rensberg, who was regarding him in monumental surprise.

"It was plain self-defense, Sheriff, s'help me."

Boyd dismounted stiffly and went toward the barn opening. Sue heard his spurs and ran into his arms.

Boss Rensberg lifted his old eyes from Plover's sweaty, anxious face to the blending silhouettes in the yard before the barn. He leaned forward in the saddle, squinting mightily. His voice was garrulous.

"Say, Boyd! What the devil are you doing, boy?"

He got no answer until Powell Plover, rubbing his sweaty palms together, looked at the lovers, then back to the old man.

"Oh, well. That's a sort of self-defense, too, I reckon, Sheriff. He's kissing her."

Sheriff Boss Rensberg looked down at the rancher, stunned, then slowly gazed back at the man and woman again and began to wag his head back and forth like a bewildered buffalo bull.

"I'll be damned. Completely and miserably damned. Powell, things're changing, boy. World's getting too complicated for me. Used to be women, horses, and cattle a lawman had to figure as the root of trouble. Now it's women and gold and smuggling, then horses and cattle, I reckon. I'll be damned."

The Dark Trail

I

Will Brennan rocked easily with the motion of the stage. His wide-brimmed, black hat, tilted a little away from the broad width of his forehead and the solemnity of his blue eyes, nudged the rolled curtain when coming into contact with it under the rocking motion of the old coach, battered and blistered from long use in a dry, hot land. Will watched the gigantic sweep of the frontier roll up, shimmer before his eyes in the heat, hesitate, then flee rearward, making room for the next panel of view. It had been like that ever since he had left the barracks, a civilian again, his body covered with stiff new clothes that felt nostalgically familiar and strange, too, at the same time.

His heart beat faster when familiar landmarks came up, danced before him in silent welcome, then slid away for the closer, more intimate recollections they stirred, to roll in a vague grayness behind his eyes. The palms of his broad hands, where they lay in his lap, were sticky with anxious perspiration.

Cottonwood was close ahead now. The fading light of a sunburned, brassy summer day was dying, mellowing the vistas and softening the memories. Will could close his eyes and see the vivid little trail town with its warped siding and manure-stained road, its sauntering men with their holstered guns and dusty boots, their bronzed faces, squinted, alert eyes, and leeched-out frames. It was a bedraggled clutch of ugliness, a series of little stores knocked together, literally forced into one another's arms and leaning into one another for support in the hostile violence and natural brutality of the frontier. But it was home to him, and memory softened it, gentled it, and served it up benevolently at the close of an insufferably hot day, rounded and cleansed and shadowed to hide the meanness of it, as it came back slowly, far ahead of the sweating horses that were drawing him back to it.

Will was conscious of the other three passengers like a man will be, conscious of other presences enough not to bump them, but totally unaware of them as people. He didn't see the sloe black eyes of the beautiful girl watching him from the far side of the massive, bulky man with the iron-gray moustache. Although Will did not know the girl, she knew him. In absence many things change, but young girls bud more quickly than anything else. They emerge and blossom and ripen, and wait, like Annalee Burch was doing, and, while others marvel at their beauty and transformation, only they themselves know fully that they have emerged, and what they are waiting for. Annalee knew, and her unblinking study of Will Brennan was the best key in the world.

She was admiring the almost sad look he had, the whipcord hardness of his body, the accumulated little lines grown deep and lasting around his blue eyes, his fine, large mouth, and even around his squared jaw and its blunt swelling of chin that protruded below his nether lip. Annalee approved sincerely of what she saw, and it was poignant, too. For two reasons. One, Will, whom she had known before the Army had swallowed him up, had looked at her when they had boarded the stage—and through her. There had been no recognition at all, and it had hurt. And, two, because she knew something that Will Brennan couldn't know, for, knowing, he never would have returned to Cottonwood. She knew that Will Brennan's reported death in Johnson's Army, before the very gates of the Mormon Zion at Salt Lake, had driven his wife into an awful mourning for two years. Then she had re-married and now lived on the old Brennan Ranch six miles from Cottonwood—with her new baby!

Will's head was filled with an oft-repeated song he had heard a saint in Brigham Young's army sing after Johnson's men had swung through their deserted capital:

> When Johnson's army comes
> We'll drown 'em in the lake,
> And leave their bones
> To bleach upon the sands,
> On the sands!

It brought a faint, sardonic little twist to his mouth as had the readying of the great army at Fort Leavenworth, the rabidly anti-Mormonism of not only the States but of the entire frontier, and his own indifference to it, in fact, of his own forbidden reflections on the intolerance of the Gentiles themselves, and the way their intolerance spread like a sickness. They who claimed all men were entitled to freedom of worship. He shifted a little on the jouncing seat and thought of the near-battle that had occurred when Utah Territory's militia—the Nauvoo Legions, the Mormons had called it—had rushed out to meet General Johnson's force, been astonished at the size of it, and had fallen precipitously back on their capital, Salt Lake City.

Will's mouth held its ironic twist. There had been the war of words then, in the autumn. Later on, the bitter cold and the war of maneuvers, sniping, raids, burning and looting of each other's supplies, before the Mormons had fallen back again, resigned their capital to destruction which Johnson refused to accomplish, and finally the entire fiasco was left to dwindle and die and fall apart until Will had spent his final year in blue in a Leavenworth barracks, tolling off the time until he was this close to Cottonwood and the bride of six months that he'd left behind on the ranch he had bought with the money saved as an independent trader on the Santa Fé Trail.

Annalee Burch knew all this, too—all except the suffering of the winter of 1857 before Zion, and the murderous monotony of the fort at Leavenworth. She finally looked away from Will's handsome face. A shout had gone up from the driver. She leaned a little and looked out her window, saw the heat-ridden little town of Cottonwood with its shaggy, life-saving cottonwood trees shading it looming ahead. Without complete awareness she nudged the massive man next to her, twice. The second time he opened his eyes and closed his mouth simultaneously, blinked moistly out at the sun blast, squinted, and averted his head under the whiplash of painful brilliance, and mopped the residue of perspiration that hadn't been absorbed by the limp collar around his columnar neck.

"Comin' in, honey?"

Annalee answered with a little nod, without looking at the man. Their eyes were identical, jet black and wide set, large and beautiful, even in the man, Jerem Burch.

"Yes, Pa. We're coming in."

Burch changed position slightly in the seat and sighed. "Be sundown directly," he said pointlessly.

Annalee smiled up at him. Her face was exquisite with its creamy coloring. "Yes, by the time we get home it'll be dusk."

"I hope Ellie's got the rig waiting."

Annalee's eyes wandered, settled on the brooding look of Will's profile, caught, and stayed there. "Oh, I'm sure she will have, Pa."

Jerem Burch nodded. "I reckon she'll be there, she and

some of those bucks she's running with."

Annalee's eyes left Will's face for a second, searched her father's blunt, honest, slightly impatient features for a hint of what prompted the remark about her sister's friends, then went back to Will's face again. She didn't worry about Ellie.

Her sister was capable, too capable sometimes, it seemed to Annalee, like granite, and yet unfathomably restless. Ellie had the same robust beauty, the ampleness of figure and strength, but there was something unknown, passionate, and savage in her, too, that Annalee had never understood. But she wasn't worried about Ellie right then. It was Will Brennan and what would happen to him when he saw his wife married to another man, with that other man's baby in her lap, that held the girl in a grip of suspense. Fear, almost.

And she decided to act. The conventions that had raged at her ever since the lean, changed man had come into the coach and she had recognized him shrunk from what she was thinking. Her conscience, too, writhed unhappily. She didn't want to hurt him. She didn't want any of them to suffer, and, her business or not, she made the decision and was the first to alight when the coach whirled to a noisy, dusty stop in the gathering twilight.

Will breathed in the fragrance of the little town. His eyes took it all in again and placed it vividly back in his mind without the gray vagueness it had had for the past three years. It was good to be home, to belong again to something tangible and friendly and environmentally understood. He had never belonged in the Army. He belonged on the frontier. In Cottonwood.

"Mister Brennan?"

Will turned, agreeably startled by the feminine voice, and looked down into the ebony eyes. They were familiar eyes, and yet not so familiar, either. He smiled. "Yes'm?"

"You don't remember me. Annalee Burch?"

He remembered the name and, vaguely, the gangling, sturdy girl. It was a shock, as it always must be, to see beauty where awkwardness had always been before. He didn't hear the voice again until it had almost stopped.

"Would you . . . please . . . for just a moment . . . ?"

Will's face still held the pleasant, subdued smile of contentment. "I'm sorry, Annalee. I wasn't listening. You've changed so. You were. . . ."

"I know. Please, will you walk down toward my house with me? I want to talk to you. Please?"

He threw a glance at the twin, untrimmed wicks of the carriage lamps on either side of the livery barn doors, hesitated, felt the pressure of her hand turning him away, shrugged a little to himself. It wouldn't take long.

Nor did it.

Annalee watched him, afterward. There had been a choice of ways. She had taken the direct route. It was blunt and frank, succinct and cruel. The other way would have been prolonged, diplomatic perhaps—but just as cruel. She watched the blankness creep up slowly, until it found a footing around his fine blue eyes and settled there. She said nothing, but instinct made her reach for his big hand and hold it in both of hers. The darkness made his face unreal-looking in its blight of shock, with the color gone and the lines deepened. She squeezed the hand, hard. He needed something right then to grasp and hold on to. She offered it, but the hand she held was limp and cold. It made her think bitterly that this man had given *more* than life for his country.

Will finally looked down into her upturned face and smiled in an ill-looking way, then nodded. "Thanks, Annalee. You did right. All that talk about it not being your business . . . was wrong. I appreciate it, too. They would,

56

also, if they knew. Tell me . . . what's his name?" Before she could answer, though, he shook his head quickly. "No, I didn't mean that. I don't want to know. Just tell me this. Do you see her often? Is she happy?"

Annalee nodded. She saw Beth fairly often now, every few days in town, and she *was* happy. Jim Ball, her new husband, was a good fellow. Easy-going, maybe a mite lazy and weak not to aspire to anything more than the ranch Beth had brought into the union, but he was good to Beth and their little daughter, Carey. She was a spitting image of her mother, too.

"They're happy, Will. All three of them."

He nodded again, brusquely, feeling the pain creep in over the paralysis that had come first, then he sighed. "Well . . . thanks again, Annalee." He didn't say good bye, just withdrew his hand and walked toward town, the dull *clump, clump* of his boots on the plank walk like measured beats of a muffled drum.

Annalee stood there, just off the sagging old porch, listening to the drum roll of his steps in the darkness. Other sounds filtered into her consciousness, too, like Ellie's laughter in the house, where she and Mart Beacon were listening to her father tell of the awful trip to Livermore and back, and the sounds of Cottonwood coming out to stroll and roister in the cool night. But only one sound stayed in her head. The somber tread of Will Brennan going—somewhere.

She started to run after him. People looked, shook their heads, and went on. The anxiety was lost in the gloom for none to see, but Annalee wore it like a mask until she came up even with him near the livery barn doors, where he was looking at the twin lamps with the dirty, moth-littered chimneys and spiraling little freshets of oily smoke.

"Will, where are you going?"

"Oh," he said quietly, indifferently. "I . . . don't rightly know, Annalee. Away, I reckon. Wouldn't you?"

She nodded, wanting the worst way to put her head on his shoulder and cry—and make him cry, too. "But where?"

For the first time his eyes focused directly on her, like they had when she had spoken to him, introduced herself when they had gotten down from the stage. Then he shrugged, making that unpleasant little smile again.

"Well, I don't know as it makes much difference. I might go to . . . let's see . . . I knew some Mounted Rifles from California. I might go there. Or Arizona. They tell me that's a lot like New Mexico, here. A man can do things there, I've heard. Big things, Annalee. Maybe that's where I'll go."

She knew what he was doing but had no experience to combat it. She had come to know men a little, but not under circumstances like these.

"Will . . . I want to ask you to do something for me. Will you?"

The smile broadened a little in his eyes. "Now, Annalee, how can I answer that? I haven't any idea what you mean."

"Just promise me you'll write. That's all. Will you?"

He was silent for a long, painful moment, regarding her, then he nodded carelessly. "All right. But I don't think it's a good idea."

"Why?"

He noticed the wide way her eyes were set and the fullness of her underlip. "It won't do any good. I don't want to think of Cottonwood, Annalee. This is unpleasant for you, too. We'll just be keeping it alive."

"But, you'll promise?"

He almost laughed. It was a dry, rasping sound like a blacksmith's file going over an unshod horse's hoof. "All right. I'll keep my word. But nothing was said about how often."

She stood there looking at him, seeing the small warning flags of annoyance coming into his eyes. She stepped aside, nodded once, and walked back the way she had come. Just once, before the night blotted him out, she turned and watched him enter the livery barn and walk over to the little door where you bought stage passage. The ghostly light from the uncared-for carriage lamps limned him, broad-shouldered, tall and rock-hard, the black hat back a little on his head and the shiny tip of his pistol holster showing slightly below the hemline of his coat.

The blow was one of those near-fatal things that couldn't be absorbed all at once. Will was still feeling like he was high on a hill, watching this happen to another man and his wife, but all the time he knew it was Will Brennan it was happening to.

"Where to?"

"Oh . . . Arizona, I reckon."

The night man looked up quickly, closely, then his dry answer came back softly. "Well . . . she's a big territory, stranger. Got to deliver you somewhere particularly, you know."

Will felt the sting, looked squarely at the man, and tried to remember the name of some town in Arizona. He couldn't. "You ever been in Arizona, pardner?"

The man looked even more startled. "Well . . . yes. As a matter of fact I have. Come to New Mexico from there just two years ago."

"Where's there a good ranching country there, with a river maybe, and a good little town and maybe some shady trees and. . . ." It died there. Will became aware of the incongruity of what he was doing and blushed.

The clerk smiled at him. "That sounds more like heaven than Arizona, stranger, but I come from a little place sort of like that. Good grazing land and a river, trees, too."

"What's it called?"

"Havasu."

"Good. I like the name, too. Make me out a passage to Havasu, Arizona."

He waited in the shadows of the livery barn, suddenly afraid someone else might recognize him, although he had changed a lot. Still, if the Burch girl did, others might. He made a cigarette and smoked it alone in the dingy gloom of the pungent old barn. His mind went back to Annalee Burch. He got a jolt then. What if *she* told? He considered it thoughtfully. She certainly didn't seem the type. Still, you couldn't ever tell. She *was* a woman. He spat in his palm, made sure the cigarette was out, dropped it, and looked at his watch. The stage wouldn't be in, horses changed, and ready to roll again for more than an hour. He sighed and walked out the back alley of the building, swung south, and headed among the refuse piles toward the Burch home.

He stood in the shadows, wondering how to get the girl to come out. Her father hadn't recognized him on the stage, but that didn't mean he wouldn't recognize him under a lighted lamp, now that he was wide-awake. Besides, he remembered Annalee's older sister. Ellie would recognize Will Brennan right off. She had been a close friend of Beth's before and after the marriage. He thought of Ellie irrelevantly and wagged his head. She was beautiful. More handsome than Annalee, but she was so violent, so domineering and strange and, well, just plain unpredictable that Will had never cared much for her.

Then the dog started to bark in the yard next door to the Burch house, and Will had an idea. He opened the back gate, let the animal out, and pretended it was chasing him. The dog, a small, frowsy animal, was delighted and ran after him

60

barking and snarling viciously. It worked better than Will expected. Ellie came to the back door, peered out scowling into the night, and told the dog to be quiet.

"Ma'am," Will said huskily. "Would you ask Annalee to come to the back door, please?"

He held his breath, watching Ellie. Her beautiful features altered in surprise, stayed motionless for a moment, then fell into a scornful, pleased look.

"Sure, just a minute."

Will went close to the grape arbor, ignoring the little dog that grumpily waddled back to his own yard, bewildered, and waited. Annalee stood framed in the orange lamp light from the kitchen, looking out uncertainly.

"Annalee? It's Will Brennan."

She closed the door behind her and came toward the voice. He took off his hat this time and the faint glow of lantern light shone coppery in it.

"Yes, Will?"

Looking at her, he felt ridiculous. She wouldn't talk about his return. It was foolish, what he had done.

"Will? What's the matter. Why did you come back?"

"I wanted to remind you . . . please, miss . . . not to talk. Not to say anything about recognizing me. About me coming back to. . . ."

"Of course not, Will. You didn't think I would, did you?"

"Well," he said evasively, "I just wanted to make sure."

"I won't. You have my word on it." She was close to him in the shadows. The scent of lavender went out to him faintly. "I wouldn't have anyway."

"No, I don't reckon you would have," he said lamely. "Well . . . good bye again, Annalee."

He was too startled to move. She moved fast; the fragrance was heady when she was against him, searching for his mouth in the darkness, and he kissed her instinctively, still too dumbfounded to react normally. Not until the salty taste of tears on her mouth made a tangy bitterness that found response in his own feelings, sobering him, did he take his arm from around her and push her away.

"Annalee . . . there was no call for that."

He was stern, thinking that she was going to be like Ellie, wild and sort of abandoned. He pulled his hat on in one swift movement and moved around her, heading back down the alley toward the livery barn again.

Annalee sat down in the arbor and pressed both hands over her mouth. She hated herself. Why had she done it? Because she felt sorry for him? Partly. But something else made her do it, too, and, whatever it was, she couldn't have picked a worse time. She knew that, too. Any woman's kiss to Will Brennan, right then, was bound to be acid. She put her head down and cried, feeling ashamed and wicked and unclean.

II

Annalee Burch was the only thread that held Will to Cottonwood, and that single thread was so thin, so intangible and weak, as to be nearly non-existent. He had been in Havasu, on the desert's fringe, for about five months, a deputy sheriff whose reputation as a bounty hunter was fast growing into legend. And when he returned tired and dusty from a successful pursuit, the forlorn captive tied to his bony nag, another deputy, a man named Clem Everest, saw him tie up before the adobe sheriff's office and went out to meet him.

"See you got him . . . good. Got a letter for you."

Will's alkali-encrusted eyelids widened in disbelief. "For me? Hell." The bitterness that was so much a part of Will rang in his voice. "It's a mistake."

Deputy Everest, taller than Will Brennan but not so compact or sturdy, shrugged and looked beyond the bounty hunter at the wasted man on the led horse. He shrugged. "It's got your name on it. That's all I know."

He handed Will the bedraggled little envelope indifferently and jerked his head at the prisoner. "This John Tracy?"

Will didn't answer. He was looking at the letter like it was a severed head.

Everest turned a critical stare at Will, saw the expression of dread on his face, and turned on his heel to untie the prisoner, the silent scarecrow that Will Brennan's tenacity had run to earth, fought to a standstill, and brought back to Havasu. He helped the man dismount and supported him.

Will had the envelope open and was reading the letter when Clem Everest and the horse thief, John Tracy, went past toward the office. Everest's glance was sardonic when they passed Will. He was dehydrated, almost ill with exhaustion and weariness, but he stood beside his horse in the boiling sun, a ragged, unwashed manhunter, absorbed in a letter and blind to everything else.

Will's mouth pulled in flat against his teeth as he read. The hollows under the blue eyes, with their haunted restlessness, made an evil shadow that changed the expression completely. The whisker stubble and alkali dust, the split, swollen lips with their seams of dried blood, and, finally, the dull, unblinking savagery in the depths of the eyes themselves—Will Brennan was a different man.

He stuffed the letter in his pocket, grunted to himself, and untied the horse. The animal was red-eyed and gaunt with a listlessness that came from hard usage. Will took him to the livery barn at the north end of the town and handed him to the wide-eyed hostler, who was one of those to whom the growing legend of Will Brennan, manhunter, was becoming a saga of almost unbelievable proportions. The man risked a question. It was common knowledge that Will had gone after the notorious horse thief, John Tracy.

"You get him?"

Will regarded the man for a space of five clock ticks, saying nothing, then he turned on his heel and walked out of the coolness, crossed the dusty roadway, stepped up on the gray duckboards on the opposite side of the road, and hiked south until he came to the Federal Eagle Saloon. Here, the smells of the place were familiar and pleasant, a sort of coolness based on masculine likes: whisky, sweat, sawdust, and tobacco smoke. The day barkeep knew him like everyone else in Havasu did, to nod to, and answer as briefly as possible.

"Bran mash, Stan."

The barman nodded, made the drink, and took it to Will. The letter was lying flat on the bar top, smoothed out with dirty, weathered hands and held there, like a man would hold a child's face while he peered down into it. Will read it twice more. The words came off the page and hit him. They were simple, direct words, honest and blunt, like Annalee would make them, as she had been the night she had told him about Beth, the new baby, and the husband. Carefully he folded the paper, put it in his wallet, and looked at the stuffed eagle over the bar, poised for flight on its perch, fierce little glass eyes fixed on something far off, above the earthiness of the saloon. He downed the drink and slammed the glass down, waiting. The barman filled it again, shooting a questioning look at Will.

"You get him, Will?"

Will looked at the heavy face with its melancholy eyes, its handsome black moustache shot with gray, and the look of quiet tolerance on the strong features. He downed the second bran mash neatly and handed the glass over. The third refill came up before he spoke. The fire was coursing dully in his veins by then.

"Yeah, I got him. 'Way out near Apache Peak. Rode him down." The blue eyes were fastened levelly on the barkeep's white face. "John was a tough one, Stan . . . if it makes you feel better. He tried to stay in the hardpan sink so's I couldn't track him, then he shot a hole in the cistern at Indian Wells, and finally he turned back and tried to dry-gulch me."

"And you got him." The voice was flat, with a definite matter-of-factness to it.

"Yeah. And I got him." The third bran mash went down, and the glass, getting a little sticky with unhealthy sweat now, was refilled and set up again.

"Listen, Stan. Maybe we look at things differently. I should tell *you* I'm sorry, if I tell anyone. He's your brother. But I'm not sorry, Stan. John is a horse thief. An outlaw. You know it, and I know it."

"I didn't say anything, Will."

The manhunter's grimy black hat bobbed once gently. "I know you didn't. It's just that you've got a right to know how I took him, is all."

The barman's eyes held to Brennan's face, flushed and ill-looking and sweaty. "Yeah. Younger brother, Will. I reckon everyone fails now and then, but . . . I'd sure have given a lot not to have failed with John." The man started away, drawing a sour bar rag from his apron.

Will's vision was getting fuzzy around the edges, but his mind was still clear. "Wait, Stan. You didn't fail with him. He's a grown man. Every man makes his own choices, right or wrong."

Stan's face, without anger but certainly without friendship either, turned a little. His eyes held to the oily, unclean features of Will Brennan.

"And . . . you're right, Will?" He didn't wait for an answer, just shook his head. The movement told his thoughts far more eloquently than the words that followed. "I wouldn't have your job for a million dollars."

Will smiled crookedly. "No, I don't guess you would. But five years away from Havasu might make John think a little, Stan. Prison might do what you couldn't do. Make a man of him. Another thing, too. He came in alive."

Stan's eyes were sardonic, but he said no more. There was nothing more to say anyway. He nodded slightly, staring at the bloodshot eyes across the bar from him. "Want another one, Will? On the house," he said dryly, "for not killing the kid?"

"Sure. On two conditions."

"What?"

"You sell me a bottle of rye whisky and let me sleep in the storeroom again tonight . . . and your word you won't slit my throat after I pass out."

The barkeep didn't answer right away. His glance was steady and even, again neither pleasant nor unpleasant, like the look a man uses when he sees a rattlesnake beyond rifle range.

"All right, come on."

Forgetting the free drink, Will took the rye bottle with him, went past Stan's motionless form beside the storeroom door, and tossed his hat on a shelf before he turned, nodded sardonically at the wooden-faced barman, and sank down on a crate of liquor. He set the rye bottle down carefully and raised his unhealthy-looking face, greasy, weary to the bone, and nodded once dourly. "Good night, Stan . . . and thanks."

Stan straightened, nodded his head ever so slightly at the filthy, ravaged man as though he wanted to say something, then turned away and closed the door.

Will stared at the floor and began to wag his head back and forth, back and forth. The words came to him verbatim. Even the handwriting, small, graceful and uniform, was behind his eyes. *You said you'd write. I think I know why you haven't, and I'm terribly upset about it, Will. Awfully sorry. I don't know what caused that, but I know we'll never forget it . . . at least I won't . . . so I can't suggest that we do. About all I can say is that I'll never mention it again, unless you ask me to.*

Anyway, that's not why I'm writing. If I could talk to you, maybe I could say it better than I write it. Jim Ball was Beth's husband. You didn't want to know his name, but now you'll have to. He robbed Pa's bank in Cottonwood, killed old Carr Carter, Pa's oldest clerk, and rode off. Beth is gone, too, but Pa says the sheriff here doesn't think she went with him. He had her traced—she and the baby, I mean—as far as Independence, Missouri, and lost them there.

I'm writing this so you'll know your ranch is deserted and maybe you'll come back. Maybe Beth would've stayed, too, if I'd told her you weren't dead. She left before I could make up my mind what to do, Will.

Maybe if we'd gone out there together, that night you came to Cottonwood from the Army, things would've been different.

If you're wondering about the address, I asked the stage clerk at the livery barn, where you had gone. He told me. Will . . . please write.

He reached for the rye bottle, saying her name aloud. "Annalee Burch. Maybe this, maybe that. The banker's pretty little daughter. Used to be all legs and big black eyes. Little Annalee . . . but maybe she's like Ellie, and, if she is, she's no damned good, so to hell with her . . . and Ellie, too." He twisted savagely at the bottle cap. "And this Jim Ball that Beth married." He laughed and spat. "Well . . . he's one I can't hunt down very well, can I, Beth? To hell with him and his reward then. There's plenty others. Let him stay over in the Cottonwood country. Arizona's got more'n her share of outlaws anyway, and I'm getting rich off 'em, too."

He shook out of his boots, stared stupidly at the holes in his socks, wiggled his toes, and swore sulphurously at them. The rye whisky didn't taste good to him, but it helped dim the memory of Annalee's letter and the knife blade in his entrails that twisted each time he thought of Beth.

Will lay back and pushed the bottle away. It made him sick to think of drinking now. He closed his eyes and thought of Beth. Pretty little Beth, so thrilled that her man would be a soldier. So naïve and starry-eyed and young. It was the poignancy of how she had ruined her own life and Will Brennan's, unwittingly, that made him curse her through cracked lips grown unwieldy and thick with the rye whisky. Then he slept.

Sleep brought Will something else. A pale parade of outlaws, stony-faced, who looked down at him. He recognized them and sneered. He had no fear of death, and they did have. So did the other lawmen who had ignored them or looked the other way, or had half-heartedly gone out after them. That was the difference.

Will's sneer died. Annalee was in front of them, and she was regarding him in the same frightened way, as though she was looking at something unearthly, unclean, and mercilessly deadly. He saw her glance drop to the dull, battered star on his filthy shirt, then raise to his face again. She was shaking her head softly at him. But when she reached up with one hand and rubbed bitterly with it across her mouth, trying to wipe away the stain of the kiss in the grape arbor, he awoke and lay there staring through a blinding headache at the ceiling, without moving a muscle.

There were muted sounds outside. Will knew it was dark and the Federal Eagle was filled with cowboys, townsmen, freighters, and travelers that congregated before the bar. The noise came and went inside his head, in rhythm with the ache. He sat up stiffly, felt the stickiness of his dirty body, and reached for his boots.

The door opened silently and the panorama of revelry lay before him in a fog of smoke that almost obscured the stuffed eagle overhead. Without looking again, Will turned, stalked toward the rear entrance, and went out into the cluttered alley, breathed in some of the cool, rich night air, and hiked deliberately toward the tonsorial parlor. The place was crowded with riders and freighters. They looked up when he entered, letting the words shrivel until he had gotten the soap, towel, and key wired to a small shingle that entitled him to a bath, and disappeared beyond the bathroom door, then the voices arose again, dwelling on the phenomenal luck of manhunter Will Brennan.

Will's headache abated, but it was still there. He bathed slowly, scrubbing himself clean, then re-dressed methodically, making a face over the salt-stiff clothes he had to put over the clean body. The knock on the door make him look up irritably.

"Well? Can't you see someone's in here?"

"Will?"

"Yeah." He hesitated, looking at the panel. The voice was familiar. It belonged to Clem Everest.

"The old man wants you, Will. Right away."

He made a grimace at the door and was a long time in answering. "All right. What is it this time?"

"Can't say here, Will. Want me to wait for you?"

"Yeah, but not here. I'll be up in my room in a few minutes. Got to change clothes. Wait for me there."

The sound of spurs retreating in the prying silence of the listening men made Will grin lopsidedly. Havasu would give its right arm to know who Will Brennan was going out after now. He could imagine the speculative looks outside. He straightened, finished dressing, buckled on his shell belt with its sagging, lethal cargo, and walked out into the hair-cutting salon. Cautious eyes leaped to his face. There was antagonism, curiosity, fascination, and even a little awe in the looks. Will ignored them, nodded curtly to the barber when he paid him, and went out into the night again. The air was balmy with the heavy scent of the desert fringe to it. He breathed it in, feeling better, more clear-headed, almost instantly.

His room over the Federal Eagle was stuffy as he entered and nodded to Clem who was sprawled in a chair in the dark, glowering at the night beyond the single window.

"Well . . . let's have it, boy."

Clem motioned toward the window. "Open that damned thing, will you? Smells like a tomb . . . or something . . . in here."

Will crossed the room, opened the window, and went back to a chair, fishing for his tobacco sack. He was sucking his teeth, and Everest knew he had taken time out to eat before coming up. He watched Will make the cigarette with impassive gray eyes, and spoke.

"It's the Verde River Kid this time."

Will nodded without looking up from his labors. "I wondered how long it'd be before he came over this way. What's he done?"

"Well . . . the way the old man got it, he's got some boys with him and he's raising hell in general. Horses, robbery, and now murder. Killed a man named John Forsyth on the stage road north of town about fifteen miles."

"Forsyth a traveler?"

"Yeah. He was new-married. Was a little slow giving over his purse."

"Where'd the old man get all this?"

Clem watched the smoke spiral upwards toward the ceiling. "From the widow. She was right beside the dead man when it happened."

"On a buggy-seat?"

"Yeah."

"Well . . . why didn't the Kid finish her, too?"

Clem shrugged. "I don't know, unless it's because she's an invalid."

Will was surprised. "The hell!"

"Crippled in the legs," Clem went on dryly. "Funny a man'd marry a cripple, ain't it? Well . . . she's pretty as the devil, though."

"All right, men marry for a lot of funny reasons. Know anything about where the Kid went? Which way?"

Clem fished for his own tobacco sack. "The girl says he had these other gunmen with him, both young fellers like he is. She said they rode west, lickety-split."

"When did this happen?"

Clem shrugged, looking at Brennan for the first time. "Two, three hours ago, not more."

Will got up and began to rummage through the ancient bureau for clean clothes. Very methodically he changed, leaving the dirty clothes in a small pile in a corner of the room.

"Let's go. By the way, what'd you do with Tracy?"

Clem got out of the chair. "He's locked up safe enough. The old man's already filled out the reward papers for you."

Will held the door for Clem, then locked it. "Good. There's no sense in me going to the office. You tell the old man I've gone after the Kid. There's already been too much time wasted."

Everest looked at him curiously. "He wanted to see you first, Will."

They were on the plank walk outside the Federal Eagle. Will shrugged indifferently. "It'll keep, Clem. S'long."

Deputy Everest watched the wide shoulders swing away from him, headed toward the livery barn. He stood in thought for a while, then shrugged, and turned on his heel in the direction of the little adobe office where Sheriff Tim Dexter waited for his prize manhunter. It was a useless wait.

The hostler screwed up his face and shook his head at Will. "Hell, man," he protested, "you can't ride that horse out into the desert again. He wouldn't carry you twenty miles. He's plumb wore out. Let him rest for a week or so, man."

Will blinked owlishly at the hostler, considered what he had said, then nodded reluctant agreement. "All right. You're right at that. I didn't think, is all. You got a tough horse I can rent, then?"

The hostler's pained look grew worried. He knew how Will used a horse: drove the animal like he drove himself, almost to the limit. Might even go *to* the limit, one of these times. He didn't want a good horse killed, either.

"Well . . . dammit!" The man sighed, looked up suddenly, and nodded. He'd just thought of a horse all right. "Sure, I got one."

"You look like you have," Will said sarcastically. "What's wrong with him?"

"Really not a hell of a lot. It's just that he's barn-sour. If you get off the old devil, he'll cut and run for home. Barn-sour as all get out . . . outside of that, he's tougher'n a mule and too ornery to ever give up. You want him?"

Will smiled acidly. "Just exactly the one I want . . . one that's too ornery to die. Saddle him up with my rig."

Mounted on the ugly-headed, small, sour-eyed buckskin, Will rode leisurely through the night. He checked his carbine in the saddle boot as he went, then made a similar inspection of his holstered .45.

Cutting the trail wasn't hard. There were only two places fifteen miles from Havasu where highwaymen waylaid travelers. Will hunkered in the weak light like a ghostly avenger, studying the churned ground until he found the dry, dully metallic droplets he was looking for, then he swung up into the saddle again with the thrill of the hunt in him, the headache and weariness forgotten, and struck westward across the vast sweep of silent land.

It was slow going because the Comanche moon shed little light except in a general, watery way, but on the other hand Will was fortunate in the reckless, almost scornful trail the renegades left.

He rode hunched and smiling thinly. Outlaws still committed crimes in the Havasu country, but since his coming none had stayed long afterward. He stopped at a saltlick where the soft earth was dusty-dry and quick to accept impressions, and here he got his first break. One of the three horses was wearing a spreader-shoe on the left front hoof. The connecting bar of steel across the heels showed boldly in the poor light. Will went on again, but now he rode with his eyes on the skyline, searching for a hilltop. The difficulty resolved into a question of selection before he found one that suited him and toiled upwards to sit motionless at long last, looking out over the dead, eerie landscape while the horse blew himself.

The reward was miles westward. A degree or two north-eastward. Will's features were expressionless with inner thought. He reined down off the hill and swung toward the pinprick of orange light, almost unnoticeable in the far distance, which more than likely was his prey.

The moon was lowering gradually in the tattered tapestry of the heavens. The hours stalked moodily across the silent land, keeping pace with the single rider with the unfriendly eyes, and time itself seemed to pause to mark his passage, then finally, when he swung down, hobbled his horse, shucked his spurs, and slid the carbine from its boot, testing the air unconsciously before he started forward afoot, the night grew tense and brooding. He made no noise as he went, either, hoping the men he was after were across the undulating rib of land that separated him from the still camp.

The fire was a dark bed of coals that cast only a weak, dying light over the three bulky shapes that lay at random, one farther apart than the others. Will sought for the hobbled horses he knew would be close, didn't see them, and turned his attention back to the men. It wasn't important, anyway, not when he was belly-down on the ridge that protected the outlaw camp and had his carbine lined carelessly on the sleeping men.

He considered the sleepers thoughtfully, with just a trace of concentration. This was nothing new to him. Just a question of what the men would do when he fired. Which way would they run? He was sure of getting two; odds were that one might escape. In that case it would become a race—Will for his saddled, hobbled horse and the outlaw for his own animal, strayed possibly, hobbled and unbridled. He shrugged. Again, odds favored the manhunter.

Slowly the carbine came up, paused, and settled into his shoulder, and the sullen little fire chased its shadow down the barrel to his eyes. He fired.

The echoes leaped up and ran down the night. Will levered the rifle once, holding it to his shoulder and raising his voice above the turmoil that erupted down below before the sounds had died away.

"Freeze! You there . . . farthest off . . . don't try it!"

The tousled heads and astonished, still-drugged faces, puffy and swollen, were staring up at the dark ridge. Only the man a little apart from the others seemed capable of understanding instantly what had happened. His wild, dark eyes raked along the ridge, searching for Will.

"On your feet boys. No mistakes."

The two men next to the fire arose stiffly without much enthusiasm but obediently. The third man was an opaque silhouette in the gloom. He came up slower, lingering a little. Will watched him closely, sensing the antagonism that would make him reckless. The man was too far away to see what his hands were doing, then all three of them were upright. Will smiled without mirth. There was no bluster, no noise, no vehement denials, just wolfish, studied patience and slit-eyed watching. This was the old game, and these were renegades who wasted no time in prayers or profanity, hardened men living in an environment of ruthlessness that scorned trickery, wiles, and anything but gun law.

Will pressed himself flatter, knowing that death was close beside him in the night—closer, perhaps, than it had ever been before. His shifted his hold on the carbine a little, so that it bore directly on the nearest man. His eyes went down, narrowed in irritation against the weak moonlight. Two of them wore no boots, and he couldn't see the third man well enough to know. No boots meant no boot knives and at least no guns hidden there, anyway.

"Stick your hands down inside the front of your pants, boys." The men obeyed, and Will growled: "Farther. Bend over and shove." The men grunted then, bending lower, knowing they were helpless even though their guns were very close. To withdraw their arms would be fatal, so they stood like that, staring at the shiny rifles and pistols in the cured grass beside their bedrolls.

Will felt uneasy about the third man, instinctively. "You over there. 'Way over. What's your name?"

"Go to hell!"

Carefully Will stood up. The three men craned their heads and watched him. He started down the gentle incline with his unfriendly glance at the farthest man. "All right, I'll tell *you* then. It's the Verde River Kid."

The man was watching Will with a twisted look of defiance. "All right," he mocked right back, "now I'll tell you *your* name. Will Brennan, bounty hunter!"

Will didn't smile, although he appreciated the interplay between them, the harsh humor. "Yeah. That's right. Kid, you made a blunder coming to Havasu, didn't you?"

The Kid straightened a little, looking upward like a Gila monster under a rock, twisting his head a little. Will saw the vicious hatred in the man's face even at that distance. He was moving toward the silent outlaws nearest him when the Kid had the chance he'd been hoping, watching for, and went into action.

There was the faintest flash of moonlight on metal, then the wild explosion. Will started in spite of himself, swore savagely, and brought up the carbine. He shot fast, furiously, because the Verde River Kid was racing zigzag into the night, and was levering for the second shot when the Kid whirled, fired with frenzied indifference and speed, then spun and raced on again.

Will was distracted by the Kid's second shot. One of the straightening outlaws jerked erect and screamed shrilly into the night. It was a knife-edge cry that made everyone who heard it cringe with alarm and tingling nerve ends. The man threw his head far back to let out the noise. The Kid's bullet had smashed into his side.

Will turned to the remaining man and motioned him toward his threshing, dying companion. The Verde River Kid was gone into the night. Ignoring the two men for a moment, Will Brennan stared after the one man he had wanted the most, then cursed bitterly and uncocked the carbine and turned back to the scene close beside him. His blue eyes took it in briefly. The wounded man was bleeding out his life in little freshets of scarlet that looked like hot oil in the darkness. He nudged the kneeling man with the carbine.

"What's his name?"

The outlaw's face was vicious when he twisted to look upward. He didn't answer right away, glaring at the manhunter. "Rufe Blevins."

Will nodded thoughtfully. "Never heard of him. He wanted anywhere?"

The outlaw's black eyes, like coals in a snowbank, showed the revulsion he felt for what he considered the worst type of lawman in the West—the bounty hunter.

"I don't know. Doubt it. He's just a kid."

"All right, get up. You've got a long walk ahead of you."

The outlaw made no move to arise from beside the dying man, still and gasping now. "Walk?" he said, astonished.

Will bobbed his head. "Yeah, walk. You think I'm going to leave you here and go prowl the night for your damned horses? Guess again. Get up!"

The man arose stolidly. "What about Rufe?"

Will looked dispassionately at the still, bloody frame of a man in the welter of slippery blackness, and shrugged. "Leave him."

"He ain't dead."

The unfriendly blue eyes looked ironically into the hate-filled black ones. "Don't make any difference. He will

77

be in a few minutes. Anyway, the man you boys shot near Havasu *is* dead. Did you wait for him to die?" The carbine barrel reached out contemptuously and prodded the man. "Move!"

The outlaw seemed on the verge of attacking the cold, merciless man before him. Deliberately Will stepped back a couple of feet and cocked the carbine again. The outlaw's face was shiny with a film of clammy sweat. His cursing was low and bitter. It ranged the gamut from genealogical doubt to provoking insult. The outlaw finally slumped, knowing Will Brennan would rather kill him than ride back to Havasu behind him. He went toward his boots, pulled them on like a drugged man, then struck out around the land swell. Will steered him with brusque directions, then, back to his own horse. He looked at the man objectively for the first time. The tension was gone out of him and only deep contempt for his prisoner—all outlaws, in fact—showed in his steady glance.

"What's your name?"

The black eyes were lusterless now. Fight, defiance, cunning and hatred even, were submerged behind despair. He shrugged. "What's the difference?"

Will growled and swung up. "None, I reckon, unless you got a bounty on you."

"Well . . . I haven't. This is the second break I've made."

"Yeah," the manhunter said caustically, "that don't sound likely. Not when you're running with the Verde River Kid."

The outlaw turned abruptly and started off ahead of the plodding horse. He didn't look up, or even turn his head when he spoke. "I met him . . . them . . . night before last. I was on the back trail when they come up. Three're better'n one, the Kid said, so we made it three."

Will shrugged impatiently. "How much bounty you got on you?"

"None that I know of."

"Maybe you don't know. What's the crime?"

"Robbery, I reckon. Bank robbery."

Will stared at the man's back. Annalee's letter in bold, big black scroll was marring his vision. He heard his own voice speaking without understanding what prompted it. "What's your name . . . *hombre!*"

"Jim Ball."

The suspicion was kin to the shock, so Will didn't feel it as badly as he had thought he might. Still, he said nothing for a full, weary mile over the cool land, not until the irony of his capture, this time, overcame the astonishment.

"Jim Ball. Jim . . . you're wanted for murder, too."

Ball's shoulders hunched spasmodically, but his face didn't lift off the ground, and he said nothing.

Will felt hatred arising in his throat. "Murder of a man named Carr Carter over at Cottonwood, in New Mexico. You robbed the Cottonwood Stockman's Bank. Old Jerem Burch's bank, Jim. There'll be a reward for you, all right . . . damn your soul." He added the last without intending to. It was part of the phlegm of rancor that sprang, unbidden, into his voice and was built on the memories he had of this man's—his own—wife.

Ball pivoted at last under the violent, stinging tongue-lashing and its bitter tone. "All right. But at least I did it because I had to. I ain't a filthy, sneaking bounty hunter, *hombre*. No damned blood-money leech!"

Will heard the words indifferently. He was looking into the face that said them and saw the youthful lines of it. There were weaknesses inherent in Ball, but these things wouldn't be apparent to a woman. To Beth. He reined up his horse, stony-faced. "Wait a minute, Ball."

The prisoner stopped, partly turned, and looked up.

"Well?" he said evenly.

"How about your family . . . what'll become of them?"

Ball's face twisted. "I don't even like the sound of the word family coming out of your mouth. Leave them out of this."

The man's animosity bounced off Will like rain. "Listen, you . . . when I ask a question, you answer it!"

"Yeah? You got guts, bounty hunter. You and that damned carbine. You got guts!"

"Shut up! Once more . . . what about your family?"

Ball put both hands on his hips and swore at Will. He spaced each word so that it was clearly enunciated, too, blistering the lawman, lashing him until even Brennan's callousness was shoved aside by indignation, then he finished it up with a challenge.

Will moved with the deliberate thoroughness that marked him after a chase. Slowly he swung out and down, shoved the carbine into the saddle boot, and walked the length of the reins before he recalled the livery man's warning about the barn-sour horse, went back, and just as methodically hobbled the ugly beast, then straightened, dropped the reins, and went back toward Jim Ball.

The outlaw was thick-chested and heavily padded with youthful muscle. He grinned in an ugly smile, shuffled his feet a little, and jerked his head forward and downward.

"How about the Forty-Five, lawman?"

Will shrugged, pulled the handgun, and let it drop on the ground. "You want me to kneel down, too?" he asked sourly.

Ball shook his head, still grinning. "No, that'll be fine. You'll be down quick enough."

Will didn't deign to answer, just advanced toward the younger man casually, both fists balled and hanging at his sides. Then Ball moved in warily, feeling out the stony-faced lawman, flicking fists that never quite reached his quarry.

Will absorbed two light, stinging blows phlegmatically, then shifted to the attack. He lobbed over a haymaker that was used exclusively to fool opponents with its awkwardness. It worked on Jim Ball like it had worked on other men in years gone by.

The outlaw's smile widened, became the genuine article, then he came in closer, underestimating his enemy nicely, and fired a high, yard-wide blow at Will's head, reaped a stunning blast that rocked him, and jumped back.

But Will was coming in now. He let his offence serve as his guard, slashing viciously and landing one out of every two blows. Ball panicked and ran backwards. Will kept right on, until he'd pursued the stockier man a good fifteen feet, then he stopped, sneered, and spat aside.

"No guts without your guns, have you . . . outlaw? Like all of 'em, Ball. Big mouth and no guts. Stand still. You're the one who asked for this . . . not me."

Ball cursed him half-heartedly, smarting in a dozen places, and stood his ground, legs wide and braced against the oncoming bounty hunter. Will walked forward again, about as graceless-looking as a hobbled horse, but by now Jim Ball was undeceived. Close enough, a sizzling arm flew out, caught Ball over his guard, and staggered him. Ball forgot his guard and pumped in blows like a windmill.

Only once did one connect, then Will gasped and fought against bending over to ease the eruption of torment in his nether region. Ball, emboldened, came in fast. It was his final mistake—and a costly one. With his right cocked back shoulder-high, the outlaw saw the fist flashing in at him and was powerless to dodge or guard against it. The world came apart and blew up in his face, sending blood-red spirals before his eyes until the blackness came up and threatened to engulf him. He felt the earth under his palms and fought back to consciousness with great effort, never quite leaving it. He was on hands and knees, looking blankly up at Will, but no boot came slashing at him.

"Get up, hardcase." The bitterness was slathered with monumental scorn. "Come on, get up. You're not hurt."

Ball got up, but his knees felt like rubber with the stretch gone out.

"Once more Ball. What about your family?"

"Nothing," Jim Ball said again, thickly this time. "Your job is to take me in. Then take me in, you. . . ."

"That's just it," the quiet, contemptuous voice said. "I don't think I will." Will saw the bewilderment spread through the glaze in the outlaw's eyes. He shook his head bitterly. "Nope. Turn around, Ball, and go back. Get your horse and ride out of the country. Don't hang around Havasu. Keep going." He was watching the amazement spread in the dark eyes. "Take a trip to Independence, over in Missouri."

But the shaft didn't hit home. Ball showed no comprehension in the innuendo. Will shrugged. Maybe Beth was on her way somewhere else. Perhaps Independence just happened to be a place she passed through *en route*.

"Go on Ball . . . slope. I'll sit here and watch you just in case. Get going."

Ball stared at Will for a second or two, then turned back the way he had come. His boots made a dull, small sound on the hard earth. His face was a white oval when he passed Will and went on, staring as Will picked up his six-gun. Will stood slouchingly, ironically aside and watched as the man became smaller as he went back where his dead companion was, and where the Verde River Kid had vanished into the night.

Off in the distance was a pale slash of light low on the horizon. Dawn was nudging into the darkness with its attendant chill. The man afoot was lost now, in the darkness. Will went back to the ugly buckskin, unhobbled him, swung up, and sat lost in thought long after his released prisoner was gone from sight.

Weariness was in every muscle of his body when he rode back toward Havasu with the full knowledge that, in the eyes of the people who knew him and his record of swift, unfailing success in tracking to earth the men he went after, Will Brennan had finally failed.

He laughed disagreeably to himself at the little town that loomed like a hunchback in the falsely lighted distance. If they knew it had been a deliberate failure, they'd be even more perplexed.

His eyes ranged over the village, its tall, shapely cottonwoods and the thin ribbon of sluggish water beyond. Havasu was pretty in a droll, pleasant, dying way, but Will thought of Cottonwood back in New Mexico with its sun-scorched buildings and bustle of trail-wise commerce and liked it far better than Havasu. Nostalgically, then, he regretted his self-imposed exile.

The hostler at the livery barn was moist-eyed and tired-looking when Will rode in, handed over the reins to the ugly buckskin, and considered the man.

"You like to have some gossip before anyone else in town has it? Ought to be good for a couple of free drinks."

The man grinned uncertainly, feeling distinct discomfort before the bleak, emotionless eyes. He prudently didn't reply.

"Will Brennan failed this time. He didn't get his man."

"Who was you after?"

"The Verde River Kid."

The hostler made a sympathetic sound in his throat. "Well, he's different. Real coyote, that one. Besides, folks can't expect a man to win every time . . . can they?"

Will looked at the man's face, recognized the forced justi-
fication for Will Brennan there, and knew the man would
speak differently at home and with his friends, and laughed at
him, turned abruptly, and went across the deserted road and
south toward the darkened Federal Eagle, and upstairs to his
room.

Havasu was silent. It was the last hallowed hour before
daylight, and even the dogs slept luxuriously, steeped in the
coldest time of the summer night, bracing unknowingly and
storing up the coolness against the bitter fury of the summer
day, then dawning.

Will thought of none of this when he unlocked the door to
his stuffy room and went in. His face was still twisted painfully in recollection of Jim Ball, Beth's husband, and the
irony of fate that had put in his hands the one man he
couldn't kill or bring in. He recalled the young outlaw's supreme confidence before they had fought. It made him grimace in contempt once more. He thought again of what he
had done, when he turned the man loose and watched him
walk back into the night.

The crowning contempt he felt for the townsmen who
would glory in the manhunter's first failure was mixed in his
look, too. As soon as the door swung inward, though, all this
vanished in a searing awareness of humanity close by in the
darkness. He stepped aside like lightning, backing along the
wall beside the door and palming his gun in a fluid, darting
movement, the hammer going back under the weight of his
thumb pad sounded loud and deadly.

III

"Will?"

Brennan's shock was complete. It was a woman's voice. He swung the gun to bear, saying nothing and waiting. The sound of skirts swishing, then the soft sound of hesitant foot-steps, confirmed what he refused to believe. There *was* a woman in his room. She had been sitting there in the darkness. He swallowed once and spoke.

"Who's there?"

"Annalee . . . Will. Annalee and Ellie. Can I turn on the lamp?"

"Go ahead, but don't move out of the window light." The thumb on the hammer gripped the dog tighter. It might really be Annalee. He thought he recognized the voice all right. The silhouette was bulky, shapely, and vaguely familiar in its full-ness, rounded abundance, and beauty.

The lamp came reluctantly to life. Orange-yellow light gathered strength and emanated softly into the room. Will's eyes banked their lids against the brilliance, and he eased off the gun, holstered it slowly, staring into two sets of ebony eyes that were regarding him in astonished consternation from across the room.

Ellie's face had a thrillingly challenging boldness to it that Will remembered well, a tantalizing beauty that invited and scorned at the same time. It was the astonishment on Annalee's face that held his eyes, though. She was looking at him with horror showing plainly.

85

"Will!"

He read everything the word implied, the way she said it, easily enough. "Changed a little, Annalee?" The smile was without humor. "A man does. Mainly, though, I've been missing sleep a little lately. A little food, some sleep, and a shave'll make a difference."

The handsome, slightly older Burch girl was shaking her head at him. The black eyes were wide in fascination and suppressed excitement. Her voice was husky when she spoke. "No, nothing'll change that face very much, Will. Not basically anyway. You know what I see in it?"

He looked sardonically at Ellie and nodded his head in silence.

She got up out of the chair slowly, never taking her eyes from him. "Bitterness, disillusionment . . . and cruelty. A lot of cruelty, Will."

He looked away from the brilliance of Ellie's glance in obvious disgust and watched Annalee. The younger girl had hidden the shock at his gaunt, savage look now. "You, too, Annalee?" He jerked his head brusquely, allowing no time for reply. "What are you doing here?" A flicker of the unpleasant eyes at Ellie. "Why did you bring *her?*"

Annalee's face didn't move. Just her mouth. "Ellie had to come. Pa wouldn't let me travel this far alone."

"I suppose he knows, too, now, he and Ellie?"

"No, Will." She said it gently, understandingly. "Ellie wouldn't have, either, if it hadn't taken that to get her to be my chaperon. It doesn't matter now, though. Beth's gone."

Will inclined his head. "I got your letter."

She seemed to be considering something, then she moved her shoulders very slightly, dismissing it. "I came to see if you wouldn't come back with us."

He laughed shortly, reached over, and shoved the still

open door closed. "What in the Lord's name for, Annalee? Are you *completely* blind?"

She shook her head. "No, but there's still your ranch back at Cottonwood. You can't . . . just desert it."

"Can't I? You think I'd live in it again?" His exasperation was evident along with the pain. "You're such a kid, Annalee."

"Will, listen to me. You're doing something awful to. . . ."

"No! *You* listen to *me*. Havasu's a long way from Cottonwood. Well . . . it really isn't. You know why? I'll tell you. In the first place, I reckon fate doesn't want me to ever be able to forget Cottonwood. Listen, I went after a renegade named the Verde River Kid tonight . . . last night. He and two other outlaws murdered a traveler who had a crippled wife. The Kid made a break, shot one of his friends, and got clean away in the dark. I took the other one. You know who he was?"

Annalee's incredulous "No!" stopped Will. It amazed him. She knew instinctively, some way, who the man had been.

He finally nodded at her. "That's right. Jim Ball."

"You . . . brought him in, Will?"

Again the dark smile. "Of course not. Could I?"

Ellie's fists were white at her sides, clenched and sweaty in the palms. "Why not? He robbed Pa's bank and killed Carr Carter. He was a. . . ."

"He was, wasn't he?" Will said sarcastically, looking at Ellie and feeling an even deeper dislike for her than he had before, a sort of repugnance. "Well, he's got a little kid somewhere . . . and a wife."

Ellie's thick eyebrows arched. "Are you the judge as well as the . . . executioner?"

Annalee turned angrily on her sister, but Will chopped her off before she could speak.

"You girls've been in Havasu long enough to listen to local talk, I see. All right, that's exactly what I am. Know why? Because I've got the guts to gamble my life against theirs. The others haven't." He shrugged again. "That gives me the right, *I* think. What you two think . . . or Havasu, either . . . doesn't mean a damn to me, Ellie."

Ellie's heavy mouth curled a little, and her eyes held to his face like they couldn't see anything else. "You *are* cruel, Will. Brutal like a wolf, aren't you?"

He didn't answer. The blue eyes went back to Annalee. "It was stupid to travel this far for such a rotten reason, Annalee."

She didn't speak, and for the first time a hint of a grin, rueful and poignant, altered her classical features a little. "Maybe, Will, maybe not. The main thing is, will you come back?"

"No! Not now or ever!"

Ellie tossed her stunning black head. "I wonder," she said.

Annalee turned on her like a tigress, the black eyes flaming into fury in seconds. "You . . . shut up! We don't need those innuendos!"

Ellie scarcely looked at her sister, but Will did. He was shocked and jarred by the barely controlled violence in the younger girl's tone and look. It shook him out of himself for a second, jolted him into a speculative appraisal of Annalee in a light he had never considered her in before.

She turned back, stared at Will with no trace of the little smile, and spoke directly to him without any inflection whatsoever. "I think you will. In fact, I *know* you will . . . dammit!"

Will's surprise remained and grew. He was looking at her, and it made him feel lost, slightly bewildered and lost—completely unaware of Beth or Jim Ball or their baby for the first time in months. He roused himself with an effort, grinning at

88

the younger girl crookedly. "Well, I'm not going to stand up what little sleeping time's left arguing with you two. Bed down here and I'll sleep over at the sheriff's office."

He didn't give them a chance to protest as he turned curtly, swung out through the door, and slammed it behind him, stumped down the rickety stairs, and stalked across the chilly predawn to Tim Dexter's adobe office. He was wide awake by then, but his body was sufficiently sluggish to let him know he must have rest. Bedding down presented no difficulties, after he'd side-stepped the curiosity of the night jailer, a garrulous old gaffer who spent his duty hours either gambling for matches with prisoners—when there were any—or drank coffee and combed his fingers through a jungle of unkempt beard by the hour.

Will didn't return to the hotel after his night's sleep in the sheriff's office. He had washed, shaved with a borrowed razor, and eaten an early breakfast before Sheriff Dexter came in. The lawman regarded him stonily for a surprised moment, then sat down at his desk and pushed the night man's forgotten coffee mug aside distastefully and dumped his hat into the cleared space before him.

"You get 'em, Will?"

"Not the one I wanted. No, the Kid got away. There's a dead one out there, though, about eight miles northwest of where the Twin Buttes trail forks with the Sangamon Trace."

"Killed one, eh?" the sheriff said quietly, his perpetually squinted eyes on Brennan's face.

"No, the Kid killed him shooting back at me." Will was stricken suddenly at the look of disbelief in Dexter's melancholy eyes. It was a rude and sudden awakening for him. Dexter thought he had shot the man down himself, deliberately. The thought grew into something else. He had to have a reputation as a wanton killer for Dexter to look at him like that, and, if the sheriff thought it, what must Havasu think?

"I filled out the papers for you on Tracy's reward."

"Thanks," Will said quickly, bitterly. "When the money comes, give it to that new church at the edge of town." He was watching the surprise in Dexter's eyes. It came, but greater than he expected. He smiled unpleasantly. "Anything wrong with that?"

Dexter shook his head slowly, thoughtfully, looking closely at the bounty hunter. "No, I reckon not. Unusual, is all."

Will stood up. "Anything else?"

"Well, I wanted to see you last night before you rode out."

Will nodded. "So Clem told me. What about?"

"We got a handbill from a town called Cottonwood, over in New Mexico. I. . . ."

"Cottonwood! That's the only town *in* New Mexico, Sheriff, did you know that?"

Dexter's eyes widened suddenly, briefly, then fell back into their perpetual squint. "I don't follow you, Will. Anyway, their bank was held up, a clerk was killed, and the outlaw's heading this way . . . westerly, anyway."

Will smiled coldly. "Thanks . . . a lot!" He turned abruptly and left the office.

Dexter looked after him. He had grown into late middle age as a lawman. Part of his success, which was strictly based on longevity on the frontier, was because he could read men. He also had another attribute of middle age, strengthened by being alone a lot. He talked to himself. "Easy boy," he said softly to the door. "You're heading for an awful tumble. You're going broncho, Will. Better get a hold of yourself."

Will didn't intend to go to the hotel, but he went anyway. Annalee was out, but Ellie was in his room. She got up when he came in and went swiftly over to him. He felt uneasy under the black fire that was in her glance.

"Will, where have you been?"

"I told you where I was going to spend the. . . ."

"No." She shook her head at him. "I don't mean last night. I mean always, or the last five years anyway."

His dislike of Ellie came up instantly. "Where's Annalee?"

"Don't change the subject . . . bounty hunter." She went up to within six inches of him. It made him conscious of the ragged, uneven rhythm of her breath and the strange, savage beauty of her features. She smiled up into his face.

"You don't like that, do you?"

"What?"

"Being called a bounty hunter?"

He didn't answer right away. He was on unfamiliar soil and knew she was master here, ruler of this strange realm of passion with its undercurrent of cruelty. It made him a little sullen, and he remembered that Ellie with her explosive, primitive passions had always frightened him just a little because he never felt at ease around her, nor could he understand her.

"From you, it makes no difference, Ellie." He said it with sulky and studied insult, but the girl only laughed at him, throwing her head back in that way she had so that her glance was almost on a level with his own, then she moved even closer suddenly, and stopped laughing.

She kissed him quickly. Will felt the pressure of her full, moist mouth forcing itself onto his chapped lips. There was a sense of unimportant pain that spun upward into his mind where a galaxy of dormant passions erupted into white lights behind his eyes, and his arms went around her fiercely.

It seemed like an eternity, but actually it was seconds. He jerked away and shoved her roughly from him. Ellie tossed her head and made that same mocking laugh again.

"How do you like a *woman,* Will Brennan?"

He didn't answer. She stood at arm's length from him, still wearing the aroused, warm look, staring up into his pale, uncomfortable-looking features like some dark-eyed, handsome symbol of destruction.

"You're thinking I like men . . . aren't you?"

Finally he made an angry gesture with one hand. "All Cottonwood knew it, Ellie."

"Cottonwood!" she said with vast contempt. "Cottonwood doesn't know anything. Not a thing, Will. All Cottonwood knows is that I tried to find a real man in it . . . and couldn't. Not a single real man in the whole herd. But I think I've found one now."

She turned abruptly and walked away from him, swung around in the middle of the room, and stood there, looking at him. He noticed that the tumult of her breathing had died down and the convulsive, uneven rise and fall of her bosom had subsided. His own sudden burst of responsive savagery was dead and ashamed within him.

Ellie's face was pale and sardonic, erasing a lot of her natural beauty. "You hate Cottonwood, don't you? I would, too, if I were you. Havasu's a good place, Will. I'll send Annalee back and stay here with you. She belongs to Cottonwood, and I don't."

Will didn't know what to say. He grasped the doorknob behind him, twisted it harshly, turned without another word, and walked stiffly out of the room and down the dingy hallway toward the stairs. His spurs rang angrily as he descended three steps at a time, then he was back on the plank walk in the rising heat of the day, standing face to face with Annalee.

"Will, come on up. I've just gotten Ellie and me a separate room. We won't be in your way. . . ."

"Why don't you take your sister and go home, Annalee?"

She was stunned by the twisted anger that glared from his eyes into her face. Gropingly she tried to bridge the wrath, but her bewilderment kept the attempt from being successful. "What . . . brought this on, Will?"

"You can't do any good here. Not for you or me . . . or Ellie. I'll go get passage for the next stage east."

Annalee's recovery was complete when she answered. The danger signals were flashing in her black eyes, too. "No you won't, Will Brennan. When I'm . . . we're . . . good and ready, we'll go. Not until."

He glared at her, hating her, himself, and, above all, Ellie. "All right, stay here Annalee, and I hope you like it. But I don't want to see you or your sister again, under *any* circumstances at all."

"No?" she said bitingly, matching his asperity with her own. "What are you running from, Will? A slip of a girl in the dark . . . under a grape arbor?"

He had to think a minute to get her meaning, but when he did, it only curled his handsome mouth downward. "That again." He waggled his head at her, eyes ironic and mocking. "It runs in your family, I think, running around kissing men when they least expect it. You're no better than Ellie."

Annalee's face froze in ashen shock as though he had struck her with a quirt. She almost staggered. A woman's rapier-like intuition cut through his words to the meaning and left his thought bare to her.

"Ellie . . . too, Will?"

But he was walking away rapidly, his head erect and angry, heading toward the Federal Eagle Saloon and a domain of masculinity where he could cope with anything that came up, seeking solace in the retreat of the angered, bewildered, and out-maneuvered male.

Stan, the barman, watched Will come across the room and go to his accustomed place around the corner of the bar, where it joined with the back wall. He went over slowly, reading the tempest in Will's face.

"Bran mash?"

"I reckon, Stan."

Will watched the barkeeper pour the drink and shuffle back with it. He had a sudden impulse to talk to someone and for the first time in his life he felt cut off from people. Twisting the glass, lifting it, turning it and settling it back in the little wet circle, he spoke. Stan looked at him dispassionately, stonily.

"Stan, you said you failed yesterday, remember?"

"Sure."

"I did, too."

"So I heard," Stan said dryly, "but there's a lot of difference, Will. I don't reckon anyone was glad to see *me* fail with my brother."

The blue eyes lumped quickly, antagonistically, to the barman's face. "But . . . they were glad I failed with the Kid, eh?"

"Some were. Not many, because he's no good, but some were."

"The Kid's got friends hereabouts, Stan?"

"No, it isn't that. He's got no friends in Havasu . . . in Arizona, for that matter." Stan didn't add anything to it. He didn't have to. Will's perception was good. That good, anyway.

"I see. But . . . I haven't, either."

Stan stood his ground, although he saw the ferocity staining the background of Will's stare. "Want me to lie to you, Will?"

"No. I reckon not. Stan . . . let's not talk about it."

The barman was looking carefully at Will's face. It was a speculative, thoughtful look. As a barman, Stan had been walking the tight rope between violence and self-effacement for too many years not to understand the features, and yet he now felt that this manhunter owed him a small something, exactly as he owed Will something in return for not killing his brother when he could have so easily and righteously. He thought it all out carefully before he decided to risk it, and probably wouldn't have then except for the confused annoyance, the bewildered uneasiness, he read in the lawman's eyes.

"Will . . . could a man ask you a question without you getting sore at him?"

The old resentment welled up. Will throttled it with an effort and nodded. He didn't know why he did it, though, unless it was because he and the barman had several little, hardly understood things in common, like their mutual failures—where they hadn't had to fail, really, except for a softness that neither would ever admit. He reached up dubiously and rubbed the side of his nose, glancing fixedly at Stan around his fingers.

"What?"

"Well, I've watched you, Will. I figure I know you about half well. There was something else behind this business of the Kid's getting away from you, wasn't there?"

Will was startled. He forgot the bran mash drink in his fist and regarded the barkeeper with a blank stare. "What made you say that, Stan?"

"Wasn't there?"

"Yes, there was. How . . . what made you think so?"

Stan shrugged his sloping shoulders. "Like I said, I've studied you. Long before you went after my brother. There's a bad crack in your armor somewhere. I used to think it was something that left you with a blind spot where a killer'd get you someday. I didn't care, either, to tell you the truth. Not until after you run John down." Stan made a tired smile. "That sounds crazy, I know, but you didn't have to bring him in alive, and I appreciate that. Anyway, I've changed my idea on that blind spot a little. Now I don't think a gunman'll get you through it."

Will squinted. "I don't follow you."

"All right. I can't explain it too well myself. Kind of like this. You got something inside that makes you a manhunter. It might just as easily have made you an outlaw, or driven you to carve out a big cow empire, or maybe killing folks for hire. It ain't that nickel badge you wear at all. That just happened to fit in. You were shook up when you landed in Havasu. That Tim Dexter hired you just happened to make you a legal . . . killer . . . is all. Somewhere, though, there's still this blind spot you got that's where you can be got to. If it ain't bullet-wise, Will, it's something else . . . the Lord knows what . . . but you got it anyway. After I saw your face this morning, I knew you didn't really fail with the Kid's gang. You ran into something out there that changed you a little. It was this blind spot you got. Like I said, Will, I've been sort of studying you." A self-conscious, small smile washed over Stan's heavy features. "It ain't very clear, is it? Well . . . that's the best I can do." The sober eyes dropped in embarrassment to Will's hand, clutched hard around the bran mash glass so that the knuckles showed white. "Drink it down. I'll get you another one."

But Will didn't. The barman's eyes widened. Will jerked away from the bar and stalked out of the saloon without a word or a nod. The bran mash was exactly as he had first gotten it. Untouched.

Will went to the livery barn and looked in on his horse.

The animal was still gaunt and tucked-up from the killing chase after John Tracy. He stood there, leaning over the stall door and watching the animal eat. The loungers within the gloomy, cool interior of the building stopped their drowsy conversation. Will grimaced at the far wall of the stall. It was always like that. He remembered what Stan said about his lack of friends. Wherever he went in Havasu, the people stopped talking and made a close study of the floor or the sky overhead, or, failing that, they talked in muted tones about trivialities with an elaborate, studied carelessness that was more obvious, almost, than the silences.

The presence of Will Brennan, manhunter, dampened any gathering he went into and subdued any talk. He turned and went back out where the undisturbed hosts of blue-tailed flies lived sumptuously off the manure piles, and rolled a cigarette.

His mind moved lethargically. The subjects it selected weren't fresh or welcome ones. It was cool behind the old building where the sun hadn't reached yet with its leeching, prying fingers.

He thought of Annalee and her interest in him. His resentment grew gradually into indignation. She wouldn't let him go, leave him alone. She certainly knew Cottonwood was torture to him, yet she persisted, twisting the dagger with each look, each word, and finally this visit. It was like she was hounding him, forcing him to face things he didn't want to face. He spat at some shiny, large flies and looked his disgust at them.

And Ellie. His body instinctively tightened at the thought of her. He felt an unreasoning, peculiar thrill that brought back with vivid emphasis the things she had said, and the primitive fire of her. It was easy to shed the image of Ellie Burch, though, because fundamentally she inspired uneasiness in him, so he turned to himself, and those thoughts were unpleasant, too.

He spat automatically into his palm, snuffed out the cigarette, and dropped it under his boot toe. It was like being trapped in a deep well. He could search each precipitate wall, but there was no escape. It was dark in the twisted maze of this mental pitfall, but he sensed he wasn't alone. Annalee was down there with him, talking in a steady, incoherent way and searching for his hand in the blackness, offering to lead him out. He swore under his breath and wrenched his mind away from the purple roll of entanglements that held him.

The solution came suddenly. Saddle up and ride away. It was that easy, on the surface. He had plenty of money—bounty money. He could ride away as simply as he had come into Havasu. Go somewhere new, far away, California maybe. Out there no one would look twice at him. He'd be just another traveler. Men wouldn't stop talking when he came up. The stigma of being a bounty hunter wouldn't follow him, and life might offer him a second invitation to find his niche, and happiness. He stood there alone, looking blankly at the immense distance that spread like an endless, parched carpeting before him, and nodded. If he rode out now, no one would know where he was going, either. Annalee couldn't follow and fling her challenge into his face again.

Will reëntered the livery barn, buttonholed the hostler, and told him to saddle his horse and hang the bridle on the saddle horn. The man screwed up his face again, got a pained look in his eyes, and shook his head.

"Give him a couple more days, Will. He's not over it yet. You handed that critter a killin' ride after Tracy. He deserves better'n you're givin' him, too. He's a good horse."

Will looked into the troubled face for a silent second, then grunted. "All right. Saddle up the barn-sour, damned old buckskin then, and let him stand ready."

He went out into the dazzling sunlight and swung south toward Sheriff Dexter's office. He could send the buckskin back from the first town he came to anyway. Havasu was alive and hurrying to get its work done before the murderous rage of the sun sapped man and animal alike.

The sheriff and Clem Everest were talking when Will entered. They both stopped and looked up. Tim Dexter smiled serenely, as though he hadn't seen Will's earlier explosion in his office.

"Glad you showed up, Will. I got a letter here from the Army over at Westport. A band of killers hit a southbound freight outfit, killed about half the drovers and a few passengers that was going along with 'em, looted an Army payroll they was carrying as well as a lot of trade goods bound for California overland."

"Well, what about it?"

Everest shot Will a sidelong glance, then fished wooden-faced for his tobacco sack. Dexter shrugged, still smiling, although the look had become a little strained and fixed now.

"Oh, not much. They wondered if we had any news of a big band of renegades in the Havasu country, evidently heading west. Seems there was a woman killed in the shooting, and she left a baby." Dexter looked past Will at an artistic arrangement of casual fly specks on the wall above Clem's hat. "No reward yet, but I reckon there will be."

Will was looking intently at the sheriff. "Where did that train jump off from . . . did they say?"

The sheriff fished through a mound of paper on his desk, adjusted a pair of hexagonal-framed eyeglasses, and pursed his lips over a letter. "Yeah. It come out of . . . let's see . . . Council Bluffs."

Will sighed, the dark premonition lifting a little. Clem Everest smoked his cigarette, looking at the sheriff, and spoke speculatively: "Yeah. I used to freight over that road. You go from Council Bluffs south to Independence, then cut sort of southwest across Kansas into New Mexico, and hit the territory about where Fort Defiance is."

Will was listening to Clem. The uneasiness was filling him again. "You know that country pretty well, Clem?"

"I reckon," the tall deputy said quietly. "Darned near lost my hair up there a few times, before the Army got strong. Why?"

Will ignored the question. "Sheriff, what's the Army want us to do?"

"Oh," Dexter said, peering over the top of his glasses, "I don't expect they hope for much." He wagged the letter briefly. "This is one of those letters they write to every lawman in the country, just hoping they'll steer someone on to the outlaws." He removed his spectacles and leaned back, rubbing his eyes. "It's just a sort of formality. It don't affect us much."

Will frowned in thought. "But how come a freight outfit to be carrying passengers?"

Clem spoke as he stamped out the cigarette on the scuffed floor. "They do that up there, Will. That's rich country for highwaymen." He shrugged. "It's damned rare, though, for a big train to be bothered or attacked. That's why folks all bunch up and travel together. Of course, we got no idea just how big this particular train was, either. Might not've been big enough to scare off outlaws, too, you know."

"No," Will said. He was thinking that the outposts had lots of women and children in them. Hundreds of each, in fact. He nodded at Clem absently, then a jolt hit him hard. Jim Ball was an outlaw. He had run the man out of Havasu country. He might have headed up toward Independence. After all, that's the route Beth had taken. Surely Ball wouldn't be a party to an attack on an outfit that carried his own wife and child. Will's knees felt weak. He went over and dropped on to the bench beside Clem. The office was silent and filled with a sudden, brooding tension. Will bit at his underlip. Ball would surely head in that direction, though. Was it possible that he *had* been in on this attack? Yes, it was possible. Quite possible. Will looked up and saw the two sets of eyes on him and frowned.

"A man couldn't hardly ride from Havasu to Independence in a day," he said bluntly.

Dexter shook his head. "Hell, he couldn't even do that if he had wings."

Everest nodded shortly. "No, but the train wasn't raided at Independence, either."

Will twisted, looking at Clem. "Where *was* it attacked?"

"Over by Thistleton."

"Oh." Will grew silent again. That was different. A man could ride that far easily with a change of horses, or he could do it more comfortably and maybe get a little sleep, too, if he made it by stage. The Verde River Kid, for instance, not only could make a ride like that, but would.

The fear within him grew into a gnawing wonder. Beth had fled after the Cottonwood bank had been robbed. She had gone to Independence. After that, the trail had been obliterated by the throngs of travelers milling at that jumping-off place from the States to the frontier. He reluctantly fitted all the parts together and came up with the leaden, sick knowledge that it could conceivably be Beth and her baby.

He tried to scoff away the suspicion, but the very possibility that she could have taken a freighting party heading down across the land toward Havasu where her husband was—or so she thought—made it creditable.

Will wrestled with himself and his thoughts for a full two minutes, fighting to reject what was growing in his mind. The silence in the office became almost unbearable to the sheriff and Clem Everest before the bounty hunter looked up at them.

"Well . . . what have you figured out?"

Dexter's face was impassive. "I don't like to send out both my deputies on the same job, or even send 'em both away at the same time, but I've been thinking it over. Havasu's pretty quiet." An ironic light shone from the eyes of the craggy old face. "She's been damned hard for a gunman to make a decent stake here for the past few months. Most of 'em know it and by-pass us."

Will was fidgeting, anxious for the sheriff to get to the point.

The sheriff saw it, but went on unperturbed. "I reckon you'd both better go. Clem and I was discussing the route before you came in, Will. Cut northward, you understand. Northward until you hit the 'Pache Trace. We figure, if those lads're heading west across Arizona, they'll stay close to the foothills. That way they always got a place to duck out of sight, if they have to. All right, you boys ride east on the Trace until you get to Pilot Rock. There's no moving critter on earth can cross the desert in front of Pilot without being seen from the top." Dexter's head inclined toward Everest. "Clem's got a spy-glass, too. That'll help a lot."

Will nodded. He had forgotten his original plan to draw his pay and ride away—not exactly forgotten it, but at least had let it slip into the limbo of his mind until this one, final possibility was examined and determined one way or the other. Otherwise, there would always be a haunting question in the back of his mind about Beth and the baby. He had to have this tangible doubt in his chest laid to rest one way or the other.

"Seems to me, Tim, we'll have to move fast. If we can get to Pilot Rock *before* these outlaws get across the Big Sink, we can see 'em. But after they get on the Trace with the foothills right beside 'em, they could ride past us and we'd never know it."

"That's it, Will," the sheriff said with a tight smile. "The whole thing'll depend on how fast you boys can get to Pilot."

IV

Clem Everest shoved off the bench, raised to his full, angular height, and stretched. "Let's ride, Will," he said simply. "You ready?"

Will got up, too, but more slowly. "All right . . . I reckon we might as well. I've got to see someone first, though. Tell you what. I'll meet you at the livery barn in ten minutes or so."

Clem nodded, relaxed again. Sheriff Dexter arose, yanked at his sagging shell belt, and faced Will. "There's no bounty money in this that I know of, Will."

For the first time since Will Brennan had gone out wearing the nickel badge of a Havasu lawman, disgust filled him. He glared at Dexter, saying nothing, then walked out of the office. "Ten minutes," he said stiffly as he passed Clem.

The deputy looked after Will and scratched his ribs with a massaging, circular motion. He spoke to Dexter without looking around to face him. "Damn. I just can't figure him out, Tim."

The sheriff laughed wryly. "Oh, I think I got him figured. He's changing lately. For a while I figured he'd be just another bounty hunter that'd eventually wind up in boot hill.

Now I doubt it." Dexter shrugged, fingering his gun butt. "He had to change, Clem. Change or get killed. Just the same I'd sure like to know what makes them change . . . when they do. Not many do, and, when it happens, I'd sure like to know what it is that makes 'em do it."

Clem yawned. "Well . . . I'm just a simple man. This kind of stuff is 'way over my head." He turned and extended a lean, freckled hand. "S'long sheriff. I'll get word to you as soon as I can . . . if I can."

"Yeah, Clem, do that. And remember what I've told you. Don't do nothing heroic. There's bound to be at least ten or twelve of 'em. Besides, this is the Army's chore. You let me know . . . if you can . . . and I'll pass it on to them."

Clem nodded. *"Seguro, amigo, adiós."*

He went out into the heat of the forenoon and glanced up just in time to see Will turn in at the little side door that led, via steep steps, to the rooms above the Federal Eagle Saloon.

Will felt uncomfortable about what he was doing, especially after he'd told Annalee he wouldn't see either of the Burch girls again. But this was different. At any rate he was wearing a defiant, surly look when he went to his old room and knocked. There was no answer. For a second he wondered if they had gone back to Cottonwood. Strangely his heart lurched dully at the thought. He twisted the knob and entered. The room was as bare and clean as it had been when he had first seen it months before. There was a note on the dresser. It recalled to him what Annalee had said. This was his room again; they had another room, third down on the opposite side of the hallway. Relief swept through him. He was surprised at it, and confused, too.

Will knocked gently, and Annalee was suddenly there in the opening, looking up into his face. Behind her Will caught a glimpse of Ellie. He hurriedly lowered his eyes from the savage challenge in the older girl's face.

"Annalee, come down to my room for a minute, will you?"

The handsome head nodded as Annalee closed the door behind her and dutifully followed him. Will stood aside and closed his door behind her, too, motioning toward a chair. She went over by it but didn't sit down. The black eyes were on him like live coals.

"Will . . . ?" she said. "What is it? You look upset."

He looked for a sign of irony or triumph in her glance, saw none, and frowned slightly. "We just got word there's a band of outlaws heading west past Havasu. They raided a freight outfit about eight miles from here . . . by a place called Thistleton."

"And," she said quietly, "you're going after them. Why, Will?"

"Annalee . . . there was a woman killed in the attack on the freight train. She had a baby with her. The route of the freighters was from Council Bluffs . . . by way of Independence."

Annalee's face was tightening as he fired his short, significant sentences at her. Her mind was racing ahead of his words, too.

"Will! You're thinking it might be . . . Beth?"

He nodded. "There are lots of women with babies, but. . . ."

"But you want to be sure, don't you?"

"That's what I stopped by here for. I know what I told you last night. That I wouldn't see you again. You or Ellie. But . . . well . . . now I want to hear what you think. You knew Beth better than I did, I think. You must've. You were friends after I left for the Army. Could it be Beth, Annalee?"

She walked slowly toward him and stopped several feet

away. "It's possible, of course, Will, but why would she be heading this way? I mean . . . does anyone know you met Jim Ball . . . released him?" Will shook his head. Annalee's black eyes blinked swiftly. "Well . . . was this freight outfit coming close to Havasu, then?"

"We don't know, but it's likely. You're thinking what I was wondering about. Was Beth coming west to meet him? A rendezvous, maybe. It strikes me as pretty likely. Do you reckon it might have been that way?"

She looked away from him with troubled eyes and a small scowl of concentration. "I don't know, Will. Beth would be capable of it, I'd say. She. . . ." The black eyes swung back, read the pain in his face, and let the sentence die stillborn.

"I made a mistake, Annalee. I should have brought Ball in."

"It's done, Will." That was all she would say on the subject. "Dare I say something else?"

He felt the surge of antagonism, exactly as he'd felt it when Stan had asked the identical question, but he didn't speak, just regarded her in silence.

Annalee sensed the subtle change in him and locked her hands together before the flatness of her stomach. "Never mind, Will." He heard the hopelessness in her voice and almost relented. "Later, maybe," she added, then levered up a pathetic little smile. "When are you going after these men?"

"Right now. I just wanted to see what you thought. A woman's ideas on the thing, sort of. You understand, don't you?"

The little smile lingered. "Will, I understand a lot of things, and a whale of a lot better than you think I do . . . or than you do yourself."

"That's a riddle, Annalee."

She smiled infectiously up at him. "That's the wrong

word. Paradox fits better."

He let his mouth respond with a tight little grin heavy with sardonic, twisted humor. "All right. Anyway, I didn't mean to do this . . . to go out there after them."

"Maybe you didn't, but now you'll have to. Uncertainty can be worse than the truth." Again the little smile came up, but now it had a lacing of bitterness in it. "Ask me, Will Brennan, I can tell you about *that*."

He stirred uncomfortably. "Annalee, will you take Ellie and go back to Cottonwood . . . please?"

She shook her head. "No, I'm sorry. If I could do it for your sake, I would. But it's because of you that I won't."

"Another paradox?"

Her face paled and the answer was slow in coming. "It wouldn't be to a man who isn't blind, Will. Please . . . neither of us enjoys this . . . let's not discuss it. Go and see if this is Beth. That's your duty. I want awfully to know, too."

He nodded.

She stood in a little closer, moving in hesitant steps toward him again. "Will? Can I ask one small favor before you go?"

He saw the look of humbled pride and trepidation in her eyes and suspected what she was going to say. It made him feel the moisture coming out in his palms. "What, Annalee?"

"May I kiss you good bye, Will?"

He stared at her, remembering the spontaneous embrace back at Cottonwood under the grape arbor behind her father's house. Oddly enough, too, the resentment and rancor that he had felt then was lacking now. It seemed that, then, the freshness of Beth's tragedy was too close to him for any woman's kiss to be anything but repugnant. Now, well, he saw the wholesomeness of Annalee Burch, standing there, the writhing anguish of her pride open and bare to rebuff, and he

107

didn't have the heart to hurt her again.

"Will!"

Her fragrance was more than compelling to him when she went into his arms. Her mouth was frightened and timid under the light pressure he put into the kiss. Shy, almost. Then her arms went up around him, pressing him gently to her. Almost reluctantly he pushed her back and felt the rusty blood come in behind his bronzed skin, and looked at the sheen of sorrow in her eyes before he opened the door, nodded quickly, and left.

Annalee went back to the little rocker in the center of the empty room, pulled it close to the window, and sat, looking out into the brassy harshness of Havasu. She saw Will stride across the roadway, stirring up little dust devils that made a furry, brown smudge around his boots. The sound of his spurs was more imagined than real. She watched a tall, lean man arise off his haunches and hand Will the reins to an ugly buckskin horse, stare, then say something and incline his head as he turned away and swung into the saddle. Will raised a hand swiftly, turned it, and dragged the back of the hand across his lips. Annalee didn't smile at his acute and obvious embarrassment. Her lip rouge was her brand, and Will Brennan had wiped it off.

She was still watching the two riders become small after they had ridden out of town, northward on the shimmering stage road, when Ellie's voice interrupted her reverie. The older sister was looking down at her intently with a crooked smile.

"Well, I see you finally had your way. I wonder how you did it?"

"Did what, Ellie?" The black eyes regarded her steadily.

"Got him to kiss you, Annalee. Your lipstick's smeared."

Annalee didn't answer. She turned back in her silence and

looked far off where two small figures were heading away from town through the heat haze. Her glance was steadily fixed on one of them. She completely ignored Ellie, feeling that her sister was poor company at this time.

Will's reaction to Clem Everest was just the opposite on the long trail they rode. He found that the lean, tall deputy was good company. The lawman's fatalistic and humorous bents were two attributes any lawman had to have on a long, hard ride—and extremely few ever did have.

They rode until the weight of the awful heat drove them into the lee shelter of a small oasis in the cracked desolation of some rocky bluffs. There was a fringe of delicate green around the tepid spring water where the horses drowsed and grazed in lackadaisical comfort.

Clem slid down in the grass under the scraggly juniper tree overhead and tilted his hat to shield his eyes. He sighed with pervading delight, resigned to the drained energy of his tired body.

"Lord! Why the devil do you reckon anyone wants Arizona, anyway?"

It was such an incongruous, ridiculous, yet not altogether irrational remark that it made Will look over at Clem's sprawled body and grin. He washed his feet in the seepage water from the spring and let them cool in the lush grass.

"I used to wonder that about New Mexico, too."

Clem spoke without uncovering his face. The effect was a muffled, muted sound. "That's where you're from, Will? New Mexico?"

"Yeah."

Clem heard the clipped, guarded way his answer had come back and pressed the topic no further. "You know, it takes a lot of different kinds to make a world, Will. A lot. But I'll be darned if I know why a man turns to robbery in a country like this, where all the wealth's been sucked out of people before they get here. If I was an outlaw, I'd go to the States and get rich. Not out here, where a man's got to ride a hundred miles and buck another man who's got a gun, too, for maybe a hundred dollars."

Will made a cigarette and lit it, letting his glance wander down the back trail they had come over. Without reason, his mind resurrected the pathos of Annalee's kiss. He turned back quickly to contemplation of the spring and Clem's gangling, sprawled body.

"You gave the answer to that one yourself. It takes all kinds to make a world. On the frontier a lot of men start out ranching, for instance." As he talked, it dawned on him that he was unconsciously stating his own convictions about Beth's husband. "Not every man can succeed out here in cattle. They fail, Clem, or they get into a jackpot where they've got to get money in a hurry. There's only one way. With a gun."

Clem sighed loudly, shoved his hat back onto his head, and straightened up, fumbling for his tobacco sack. "I reckon," he said indifferently. "But they're going a little far when they get together in tribes, kind of, like these men we're looking for, and attack regular freight trains. Wouldn't you say?"

"Sure. But did you ever see two men who worked the same way at anything that didn't try their hands together, sometimes?"

Clem shrugged. "Never noticed."

Will reluctantly pulled on his socks and boots and looked over at the horses. The buckskin was standing motionless in his hobbles, staring back over the land they had traversed. Will grinned sardonically at him. Barn-sour old devil, one slip and the buckskin would be waiting for it. He'd take out

110

for home in a dead run and leave Will stranded in a land where a man afoot would die in ten hours, if he couldn't find water. He stood up and dusted himself.

"Well, whatever makes 'em do it, Clem, they do it, and that's why we're out here. Let's ride."

The saddled up again, swung aboard, and rode off in reluctance. The sun caught them in its full blast as soon as they were away from the shade and scorched them with redoubled fury. There was little use in talking, so they didn't try. Just a waste of good saliva anyway, unless there was something pertinent to say, which there wasn't. They were like Indians in their quietness until the shadows began to lengthen and make frequent, narrow lanes of shade that took some of the curse out of their discomfort.

Will raised an arm, pointing at a huge hulk of granite far off. "That's Pilot Rock, isn't it?"

Clem's eyes ached in their sockets from the blinding glare. He raised his head with an effort, regarded the tremendous monolith steadily, and nodded. "Yeah, from up there you can see damned near the whole world, it seems to me."

"How do you get up there?"

"There's a trail around in back. Man-made. I reckon the Indians made it so's they could use the rock as a look-out. It's a natural. The desert below's as clear as a bell as far as you can see. Farther, even."

"When'll we get there?"

Clem's eyes ranged over the weary horses, heads down and plodding, then he looked up at his companion and understood why no outlaw ever escaped him. Will had that rare tenacity, coupled with an almost bottomless reserve of strength and energy that could wear out lesser men. He felt himself to be a lesser man, right then, too, because he was ready to drop from exhaustion and Will was still erect and tall in the saddle. He grunted.

"We can make it by noon tomorrow if we hit a water hole pretty quick and make our camp or. . . ."

Will glanced at him impatiently. "Or?" he prompted.

"Or . . . we can ride through the night and make it about dawn?"

"What do you want to do?" It was obvious from his tone that Will wanted to push on.

Clem shrugged. "Damned little choice. I'm about done for. We can ride for maybe another two, three hours, then I'll have to bed down."

They rode in silence for three full hours before Will spoke again. He was watching Clem's slouched, used-up frame growing more and more unsteady in the saddle.

"Clem, there's a little seepage spring up there by those red rocks ahead. I can see the green from here. Suppose you make a camp there. I'll ride on. When you're rested, you can follow my tracks and meet me at the rock."

Clem agreed dolorously, more dead than alive, and unsaddled, watching Will push on into the gathering shadows with a shake of his head. He leaned on his gaunt horse and shook his head. "It . . . ain't human, the way he can keep it up, horse, just ain't human."

It was human all right, but when Will came to Pilot Rock at the same time the sun brought one half of its huge, glaring face onto the parched, ancient land, he didn't feel human. Weariness made each step an effort. He carefully hobbled the ugly buckskin horse and left him in a little glen where the animal rolled in the coolness, freed of its accoutrements, then just lay back, too tired to think of grass or water for a while.

Will's spurs made a small, irregular trail in the grass. Their music was tiny in the tremendous silence of this far, desolate place, as he found the rock-lined, hard little footpath that led up the smooth backside of Pilot Rock.

There was a haphazard little breeze playing around the awesome boulder, larger than the tallest cliff and solid granite. Will felt almost unearthly as he stood on the wind-smoothed top and looked out over the Big Sink, the dead, gray-brown, deserted world, the desert below him. Because of a never-before experienced sensation of almost physical dizziness and weakness that filled him, he sat cross-legged and made a cigarette, lit it, and inhaled before he looked out at the monstrous panorama below him again.

Will had been sitting there a full hour, squint-eyed and motionless, using his eyes as measuring orbs of endless and eternal Time, letting everything settle into focus and perspective so that any movement, that would naturally look incredibly slow, must also be eventually noticed, when he saw what he was looking for. Infinitesimal specks in the great reaches, coming down across the Big Sink toward him with a slowness that couldn't have really been so slight. He made another cigarette, fixing the position of the moving specks on a shiny rock they were near, before he looked away, then, the cigarette going, he glanced up again. The proof was in the fact that the specks had dragged past the shiny boulder and were heading straight toward him. He sat there solemnly watching them, imbued with a grim satisfaction, wondering if Jim Ball was with the renegades using this ancient and all but forgotten trail out of the dim past of an ageless, monotonously unchanging world.

He got up, looked balefully at the specks without consciously counting them, turned, and went back down to his horse, snuffed out the cigarette in the cool earth, stomped the wiry grass, and lay down on his side and almost instantly fell asleep.

★ ★ ★ ★ ★

Neither Will nor Clem had watches, so there was no way of saying how long Will had slept when Clem nudged him with his boot.

"Well . . . have you been up on the Rock?"

Will lay flat on his back in the shade, eyeing his companion with stolid thoughtfulness, when he nodded. "Yeah. I saw 'em. At least, I hope it's them. No one else in his right mind would be crossing that desert by daylight."

"How many?"

Will closed his eyes and puckered his brows, then opened them. "Eight. I might be wrong, but I don't think so."

"Coming straight toward the trail we came over? The Apache Trace?"

Will sat up and rubbed his head. "Like an arrow, Clem. If they don't veer off somewhere, they'll go right past us."

"Good. That settles that."

Will looked at the deputy wryly. "Does it? How do you figure that?"

"We'll head right out then, and pass the word to Tim Dexter. He'll pass it along to the Army, and they can use heliograph posts to send word ahead about which way the men are going. Simple, see? The Army throws out cavalry behind and in front of 'em. Like a pincers, y'understand, and they're got."

Will's eyes were swollen and red, but the rueful smile showed anyway. "You're a good planner, Clem. You just forgot one thing."

"What?" demanded Everest.

"That we don't know for sure that these are the men at all."

Clem snorted and swore cryptically. "You said yourself they'd have to be desperate to ride across the Big Sink in this

114

weather. Who else *could* it be?"

"I'm sure I haven't any idea. I didn't say it *was* them, Clem. I said no one else in their right minds would cross the Sink, but I don't *know* that. It might be Indians for all I know."

"You don't believe that," Clem scoffed.

Will shook his head. "No, I don't, but I'll be damned if I want to be involved in sicking the Army on someone until I'm plumb certain it's the right outfit. That could make us the laughing stock of the frontier."

Clem was still frowning where he hunkered in the shade beside his resting horse. "All right, how're we going to make sure? Dexter said no heroics."

"I got no hankering to be a hero. Not when it's eight to two anyway. I tell you what we'll do. You head back down to the Trace. Go about twenty miles back, y'see, but leave that spy-glass of yours with me."

"And?"

"And . . . after I've seen 'em and made sure one way or the other . . . I'll flash you a heliograph message to that effect, using your spy-glass as the reflector."

Clem chewed a stalk of grass thoughtfully. He finally nodded. "All right. I reckon it'll work at that." He got up, went to his saddle, and brought back the brass telescope and handed it to Will with a frown. "All I got to do, then, is get on a hill that has a good view of Pilot Rock, is that it?"

"That's it, Clem. Make it as fast as you can and stay up there. I won't use the signal until I'm sure you've had time enough to make your hill."

Clem glanced up at the molten sun and flinched. "It'll take me a good half day, I expect. My horse's about done. I dassen't push him too hard." He glanced at the telescope. "Two long flashes if it's them, one if it isn't."

115

Will pulled out the glass and put it to his eye, nodding. "Yeah. Two long ones if it's them, one if it isn't. You'll have to push the horse, though . . . a little anyway. I can signal after they've gone past me, but it'll be risky. They just might be glancing up and see the flashes."

"Oh, yeah," Clem said thoughtfully. "Well, s'long, *hombre*. Remember, you'll be behind 'em. Like Dexter said . . . no heroics."

Will threw a sardonic smile at his friend and laughed shortly. "Don't worry, Clem. Just get astride and ride."

After Clem had worried his way back down out of the heights to the inferno of the shadeless Trace once more and struck out back the way they had come, Will sprawled in the shade and dozed. The same bitter thoughts were in his mind again, but there was a new sense of pathos and peace, strangely mixed, in his mind now as well.

The vision of Beth, dim and gray, since he hadn't seen her in reality for four years was obstructed by a very vivid recollection of Annalee Burch. For once he didn't try to escape Annalee's face, either. He even smiled a little. Then she smiled back at him wistfully, and then faded out, leaving just the blank unawareness that was exhaustion-induced sleep. The sun climbed to its zenith, paused, then slid a little off center, and began majestically to stalk across the faded, bleached-out sapphire heavens.

Will awoke after what he reckoned to be several hours of deep and undisturbed sleep. He watched the hobbled buckskin graze peacefully, its malevolent little eyes watching him with no sign of liking. He noticed that the animal was fully recovered from the grueling ride of the night before except for a tucked-up look in the flanks. The seepage from the little spring that lay in a rough circle of rank grass had come closer.

He bent very slowly and washed himself. It was like succor from the furnaces of hell, although to the taste the water was neither cold nor completely palatable, having a metallic, sulphurous taste. Still, it was water and it was wet. The desert asks nothing more.

He arose, took the telescope, and hiked back up the sheer trail to the top of the rock, squatted and pulled the brass thing out of itself, searching for signs of the wayfarers. Evidently the eight horsemen had been resting somewhere in the baked expanse for their progress hadn't put them as far westward as Will expected them to be. He fixed the glass on them, squinting to make out anything that might give him a clue to their identity, but the distance was too vast.

It wasn't until at least two hours later that he could distinguish man from horse and individual from individual, then he leaned forward in concentration, following the riders as they came drearily along toward him, under the big rock but still miles distant, and finally he saw one man that looked vaguely familiar.

He made a cigarette, smoked it, and put it out before he scowlingly glared at the riders through the glass again. The one rider he searched for still escaped him. The familiar figure was in the lead now. It wasn't Jim Ball, that much was evident. This man had a proud, arrogant cant to his shoulders and head that rang a bell somewhere in Will. He put the glass down, staring, and cursed to himself.

It wasn't until the men were toiling their way upwards on the trail just below him at the foot of Pilot Rock and he had flattened belly-down, the one glass eye singling them out individually, that he knew his man. He put the telescope aside, absorbed in watching the leading rider. The Verde River Kid was out in front. It could be no other. Will made a wry face and spat, having seen the sweating horses, then he stood up, turned the glass westward, and caught the sun in its oval, magnifying lens and flashed his message.

Will used the prearranged signal four times at spaced intervals. Two brilliant, dazzling flashes of reflected light bounding out into the shimmering distance like miniature sunbursts, then he hastened down off Pilot Rock, trotted to his horse, saddled, bridled, and swung up, threading his way carefully down on to the Trace where he stayed in hiding until the renegades had gone by. He let them become ghostly, wavering horsemen in the sun's crushing distance a mile or so ahead, before he paralleled their course, heading as they were heading, overland toward Havasu.

The buckskin horse sensed the direction they were riding readily enough and walked swiftly along. He was rested and refreshed, too. Will was cautious, keeping as much off the trail as he could. It wasn't likely that the Kid would have a lagging vedette; still, he couldn't be sure.

The shadows lengthened a little, casting long gaunt splotches of darker color before him. The land lost its shimmer but none of its cauldron-like heat. As often as he could, without undue strain on the buckskin, Will sought out the slight raises in the land and spied on the moving horsemen ahead. The riders seemed to be slouched and unsteady in the saddles. His lips curled wolfishly each time he saw them. The Kid's back was still erect, but the other seven men were obviously drugged with suffering and exhaustion. They all looked flat to Will in the brittle, hard daylight. There was no depth to their outlines in the shifting patterns of heat.

He followed along like a lobo wolf, near enough to hear the horses' hoofs when they dislodged a pebble or struck granite, but never so close he would alarm the riders or run more than the narrowest risk of detection.

It was well into the night before the Verde River Kid

turned off into the near foothills and made his camp. The spot was a small, narrow, blind cañon where a breath of coolness promised water and grass. Will watched the scarecrows disappear like wraiths into the gloom, then he backtracked, hobbled the fretting, barn-sour buckskin whose sole thought was home, the direction in which they were now traveling again. He shed his spurs, took the carbine like he always did when he was running down an outlaw, and moved off into the shadow world with scarcely a sound.

A long way off a coyote sounded. Will stopped, listening. There was a belated reply still farther. He moved out again, knowing the sounds were animals, not men imitating animals. He wondered where Clem was and irritably thought that the deputy would do better to stay away than come stumbling down toward the outlaw encampment in the dark hours.

There was bound to be a guard posted, no matter how weary the renegades were, unless they were absolutely confident they were safe. He twisted and turned so as to avoid what brush he could and stopped often to make sure there was no sound around him.

He hesitated just below a lean, cadaverous hogback of windswept eminence and checked the carbine as he always did. It was this application of one of his own long-standing laws of caution and prudence that made his heart go back to its normal cadence. There may have been more at stake than Will Brennan would admit to anyone but himself—and Annalee— but the pursuit, the ambushing, and the final act were all things old to him from having repeated them many times in his pursuit of bounty money since coming to the Havasu country.

V

The Kid had set up his own quarters a hundred feet from the others. This clinched it for Will. He recalled the man's unnatural habit in doing this same thing, once before. He lay on the advantage of the bony ridge and studied the camp. There was a guard who, to Will's astonishment, was not only wide awake, but alert enough to keep his eyes moving.

The outlaw horses weren't scattered, either, as he'd hoped they might be. They were hobbled and close to the exhausted men, too close for Will to risk stampeding them. He squirmed irritably, eyeing the sentry and seeing the man's head swing in his direction, rake over the ridge, and move on. There was just one consolation to Will. Jim Ball wasn't among the badly sunburned, beard-stubbled faces down below. He could see them all well enough to make out features in a hazily, generalized way. Jim Ball wasn't among them. He bit his underlip, wondering abstractly whether he was glad of this or not. For Beth's sake—yes. For the law's sake—no.

Complete darkness came slowly, twilight lingering as it does on the desert, before the grand march down the dead day by the hosts of night. Will watched the sprawled forms closely. One or two munched food from the small parfleche bags they carried, but all slept soon, and the manhunter's blue eyes gleamed like ice in the darkness. He knew how these men were sleeping. Like they were dead.

There was just one thorn in it for him. The sentry. He had to be eliminated before Will dared to crawl down and try to capture the Verde River Kid. He knew better than to try his old trick of firing into the campfire and staying hidden so that they could guess whether he was one man or a dozen. The Kid had taken that challenge once and flung it back in his teeth. There wasn't to be a second time, not with Will Brennan anyway.

He eased back off the bony ridge overlooking the outlaw camp, slid back through the brush until he guessed he was approximately even with the rocky ledge the sentry was leaning against in his vigil, and began a laborious, tedious crawl on all fours, using the carbine as an antenna to test the scrub-brush for sound before he ventured to twist his way through it. Twice he had to alter his route to by-pass dead growths that were dry enough to snap under his passage.

Will was swearing to himself helplessly by the time he emerged into the little cañon where the outlaws were. He lay for more minutes, perfectly flat on the ground and still, squinting into the weakly lighted valley. Then he saw the man.

Smoking so that the cherry red of his cigarette swelled and ebbed, the outlaw had apparently succumbed to the utter silence and seclusion of their hide-out a little. At least, he appeared far more relaxed than he had when they had first ridden in to bivouac for the night.

Will was smiling through the nervous sweat that made his face oily with its coating of trail dust and grime as he slithered toward the man. Fortune favored him, too, in that she had very considerately placed two robust mountain cypress clumps on his angle of travel so that he was hidden from the sentry, all but the last ten or twelve feet of his travels.

He made it without trouble to the last of the bushes, then risked a quick flick of his head to fling off the tickling perspiration that was running along his forehead. The sentry

stubbed out his cigarette, and yawned. He was turning when
Will eased the carbine out so that the watery moonlight reflected dully off the barrel. No one with a sense of fear and
misgiving in him could miss seeing the thing. The outlaw sentry had both apparently, because he froze, staring unbeliev-
ingly at the carbine and the vague, obscure outline beyond it
that had to be a man, and was.

Will's voice was silky-soft and quiet. "Reach around with
your left hand, *hombre* . . . just the fingers . . . and let that
Forty-Five drop."

His heart was in his mouth. If the man refused, he was in a
bad spot. One gunshot and the outlaws behind him would
come running. He held the carbine as steady as a rock. The
sentry considered the rifle, the flat shape behind it, and did
what Will had said. He dropped the gun without looking
down to see where it had fallen.

"Good. Now walk toward me and stop when you get close
to this bush." The man obeyed, and after that it was compar-
atively easy to herd him down on to the desert floor again,
nuzzle his back with the carbine, and drive him up the Trace
to where the buckskin horse was tied.

"Sit down, fella."

The man sat, and Will got a good look at his face up close
for the first time. Young, possibly five years younger than
Will, there were deep pockmarks over both cheeks and the
forehead. The outlaw's eyes were as steady and unblinking as
a snake's eyes, and about as friendly. He hadn't made a sound
since Will had first taken him. The manhunter sat down
across the way from him and leaned the carbine upright
against some rock.

"What's your name?"

"Any particular one?" the renegade asked sardonically.

"Yeah, the one that's got the most bounty money on it."

The outlaw started where he sat. Will could hear him breathing loudly, unevenly. "Say . . . you're not this here Will Brennan the Kid told us hung out around Havasu . . . are you?"

"I am. Now what's your name . . . for the last time."

"Murphy. Pancho Murphy."

Will shrugged. It was a new one on him. "You got any rewards on you, Pancho?"

"Not that I know of. I've never been over here before. Hang out over in Sonora mostly. Been in Texas a little."

Will studied the husky shoulders of the man and saw the way he was sitting with both hands on his legs that were crossed under him. He was lulled by the problem of what to do with this single member of the Kid's band and was framing the question that was uppermost in his mind right then, when Pancho Murphy moved with the speed of a sidewinder. Will was looking at him when he made the break and that alone saved him. The half-breed's boot knife was a thin bladed, two-edged little thing found more often in the voluminous folds of women's dresses than in a man's hand, but it was nonetheless deadly now.

Will rolled sideways, felt the burning sensation across his upper right arm on the outside, then he was out from under the outlaw's wild leap and kicking up to his feet seconds before Murphy came up, still clutching the little knife.

Will deliberately went towards the man, balled fists dangling. In close enough, he feinted, drew Murphy out into a wild, slashing parabola that he had no difficulty in sidestepping, aimed a high blow at the man's head, and fired it. Murphy was staggered. His hat went off as if it were jerked by an invisible wire. The knife arm was momentarily motionless, and Will elected to close with the would-be killer in that wavering, groggy instant.

He stepped in very close and brought up a low one from below his belt, let it gather momentum as it arced in under the half-breed's chin, then felt the agonizing stab of pain when the fist exploded thunderously and crashed into Pancho Murphy's jaw.

Murphy was a good ten minutes coming around. If he hadn't had a skull like a rock, he'd have been out an hour or more. Will regarded him dourly. He was holding the buckskin's reins in one hand, some half-inch wide strips of rawhide he'd soaked in a seepage spring nearby in the other hand.

"Get up, Pancho."

The outlaw arose, weaved a little unsteadily, and looked owlishly at Will.

The lawman motioned toward the horse. "Get aboard."

Murphy's incredulity was swift and overpowering. He mounted under Will's assistance, then had his hands pulled viciously backwards and tied securely with one of the slimy, water-soaked strips of rawhide. Bewildered, he watched as Will bound his ankles by running the strip of wet rawhide under the horse's belly, too. But it was the last strip Will used that finally brought home to the half-breed what Will was doing. His face was suddenly very pale as Will knotted the final strip of clammy stuff snugly around his neck.

Will reached up, looped the buckskin's reins around the saddle horn, and glanced up into the horrified eyes of the captive renegade. His voice was full of impersonal interest, too, when he spoke, and that didn't aid the terrified man's fears any.

"All right, Pancho. You know about wet rawhide, I reckon. It shrinks back to its original shape as it dries. She's a nice warm night tonight, too. Now what interests me is this . . . since you tried to knife me, among other things, I don't really care whether I'm right or wrong, either. Maybe this barn-sour old buckskin'll make it back to Havasu before the dry night air shrinks that rawhide until it throttles the rotten life out of you . . . and maybe he won't. Of course, I won't be able to know how I've gauged the tightness of the stuff until I get back, then, if I'm right, you'll be alive. If not . . . ?" He shrugged, reached up, and shoved a little folded note of paper into Murphy's shirt pocket. "Well, right or wrong, the sheriff'll find you on the horse because he's going to hightail it for home now, and he'll know who you are and who sent you. S'long, Pancho Murphy. One way or another, s'long."

Will stepped back then and slapped the buckskin on the rump. The animal twisted its ugly head, studied him from small, sullen eyes, and took a couple of tentative steps, found himself free, and walked a little way before he tried a trot, then Will saw Pancho Murphy's spurred heels go out and in suddenly and the horse was galvanized into a startled and precipitous run. Will watched them both until they were out of sight, smiling softly into the darkness. The truth was—he really didn't care either way, whether the rawhide dried first, or Pancho Murphy made it to Havasu, but he felt certain the half-breed would. He knew as well as anyone alive that Pancho's life depended on getting some place—anywhere, even a sheriff's office—where someone would cut that drying rawhide off his throat before it contracted enough to strangle him, which both he and Will Brennan knew it would do in time.

It took a good long, arduous hour to get back into the outlaw camp again, but he made it. There was a grim sense of accomplishment in him, too, when, gently, he eased over by the Verde River Kid's pallet, a sense of exultation that the outlaw leader made it a point to sleep far aside from his six remaining and soundly sleeping cohorts. Lying prone on the far side of the motionless renegade, Will raised the carbine barrel, slid it out at arm's length, and it fell lightly across the man's mouth. The barrel transmitted the quick, abrupt jerk of the Kid's body, and Will knew his quarry was awake. His voice was less than a low hiss in the star-studded silence that enveloped the black, slumbering land.

"Kid . . . don't move." Will lifted his head cautiously and threw a fast appraisal at the other men. They were beyond immediate recall. He edged in closer, took the Kid's two pistols, the carbine at finger-length from the man's pallet and the boot knife, then searched until he found a Derringer. Satisfied, he raised himself slightly so the Kid could see him, and smiled. The vicious eyes glared at him from above the carbine barrel. Will nodded slightly. "Know me, don't you?" The rabid eyes glowed their recognition. "Will Brennan, Kid. The man who almost had you not too long ago. Get up, but don't make a fast move. I'll herd you with touches of the barrel."

For all his rattlesnake courage, the Verde River Kid obeyed to the letter. He didn't speak until Will had steered him up over the bony ridge, down the other side, through the brush and dead grass, and onto the ghostly old trail that was the Apache Trace out on the desert floor. And then he didn't say anything until after Will had ordered him to squat where the lawman could watch him closely. Afoot now, Will would take no chances, couldn't with the nearest help the Lord only knew how far away.

The Kid swore ragingly until Will silenced him with a raised hand. "Shut up! I just want a couple of things from you, *hombre,* and lip service isn't one of 'em. Where's Jim Ball?"

The Kid looked thunderstruck. Will guessed he was surprised that the manhunter was interested in such an insignificant outlaw.

"Hell, I don't know. Don't care, either."

126

Will leaned from the waist. His hand streaked with unerring speed. The sound was like the distant report of a gun when the palm slammed into the Kid's face." Where is he?"

"I . . . we . . . left him." Reluctance and deadliness vied for prominence in the Kid's eyes.

"Where?"

"Back . . . there." The Kid's head jerked backwards, indicating the long trail the outlaws had just passed over.

Will regarded him coldly. His voice was dry, slow, and very sincere when he spoke again. "Listen, maybe I didn't make myself clear. I caught your camp guard a couple of hours ago and sent him to Havasu with a wet rawhide around his wrists, ankles . . . and throat. Maybe he'll make it . . . and maybe he won't. I don't care either way, Kid. I'd enjoy killing you, too. May even do it yet, I haven't made up my mind about that. You think I'm going to horse around with you." Will shook his head, adding nothing more.

"We left him back where we had a little trouble with some freighters."

Will's heart stopped beating for a second. Ball had stayed behind after the attack on the freight train. Why? There could be only one reason. Will's suspicions became a certainty in that instant. Beth was dead. It *had* been she, then.

"Kid, tell me if I'm wrong. You led an attack on a freight outfit over by Thistleton. A woman with a baby was killed. Others were killed, too. Ball was with you. When he saw the dead woman, he stayed back to bury her. Right?"

The Kid's eyes were wide in surprise. "Yes and no," he said. "Jim Ball didn't arrive until *after* the fight. The rest of it's close enough. How'd you know?"

Will sat stonily, looking at his prisoner. An awful, almost overpowering grief was raging inside of him. The Verde River Kid saw the ashen look, the stricken, glazed expression of the eyes, and frowned uneasily. He said nothing, letting the murderous silence hang over them.

Will eventually got up, took his own belt and the Verde River Kid's belt, and lashed the man hand and foot, pulling the leather so tight the Kid gasped in spite of himself. He gagged the renegade with handkerchiefs and turned away callously, ignoring the vicious glare he got and faded once again into the night.

Getting two horses, both bridled and saddled, took a lot of time. He considered bringing them back without saddles, then shrugged at his own temerity, went ahead and saddled them, too, rode one and led the other back to where the Kid was fuming helplessly.

Untying the outlaw, Will nodded curtly toward one of the horses. "Get up."

The Kid mounted with difficulty. There was not enough circulation in his limbs yet to make them thoroughly usable. Will flicked a small loop from the lariat on his stolen saddle over his prisoner's neck, took up the slack, and growled for the Kid to move out after he had mounted up. They rode through the night single-file, only the tight, hard-twist lariat holding them together, like a slender twine of destiny, which it certainly was for the Verde River Kid, and he knew it. One fast jump of his horse would stretch him his length on the desert and more than likely break his neck in the bargain.

Clem Everest had his own camp in a dry wash at the base of the hill he had read the signal from. Having slept most of the afternoon and early evening, he was drowsing fitfully when the sharp sound of a horse's shod hoofs, striking rock, drifted down the dark coolness to him. In an instant he was approaching the dusty Trace, carbine cocked and ready, looking eastward. When the horsemen loomed up, he flattened behind a dying sagebrush and waited until they were abreast, then stepped boldly into plain view, aiming at the first rider.

Will's voice made him lower the gun. "No heroics, Clem." The words rang with a dry humor.

Clem uncocked the gun and let it trail at his side. "What you got, Will?"

"The Verde River Kid."

Clem squinted up into the prisoner's face in wonder, then stepped back, looking at Will. "No heroics," he snorted, "how'd you manage it?"

"Easy, Clem. Only a damned fool sleeps apart from his pardners. Just snuck in and marched him off." Will's unpleasant glance went to the still back of his prisoner. "They all got a blind spot, Clem. First man ever made me think about that was Stan Tracy at the Federal Eagle. The Kid's too big to sleep among his common killers. He's got to sleep a little ways off from them. Air's purer, I reckon. That was *his* blind spot."

Clem looked at the Kid again. "Well . . . it may be, I don't know. What're we going to do with him?"

"*I'm* not going to do anything. You are. I want you to take him along with you when you ride back to Havasu. Give him to Sheriff Dexter and check at the livery barn to see if that buckskin horse came in, too. I'll be along later."

"Yeah, all right. Did the buckskin get away from you?"

"Not exactly. I sent him home with a man tied on his back."

"You *what?*"

Will waved his hand at the deputy carelessly. "Just check and see if they came home is all, Clem. No time for explanations now."

"Will, dog-gone it, those other *hombres* will see their boss's

129

gone and hightail it back into the Big Sink again."

"No," Will said, tossing the lariat and a pigging string to Clem. "I'll go back and herd 'em toward you. They'll come ready and fast, so don't waste any time getting to town and spreading the word they're coming, or I'll lose my bounty on this bird, you'll lose your prisoner and maybe your life, and the Army'll lose their precious outlaws."

Clem stood lost in a jumble of unvoiced questions, watching Will ride back the way he had come. He swore discomfitedly, looked up at his stony-faced prisoner, went over and lashed the Kid's legs under his horse and tied his hands to the saddle horn, then jerked him into his own camp, stalking along in bewildered disgust.

Will let his horse pick its own way slowly back toward the blind cañon where six leaderless outlaws were still sleeping like the dead.

Back once more, Will went past the cañon, swung down near the cut-off that led to Pilot Rock, and sat with his back against a skinny boulder looking up at the clear sky and its eerie emblem of eternity, the moon.

The night was well advanced and a lingering, delicate fragrance was in the coolness: the smell of parched earth and cured grass and night-blooming flowers. It was an opiate that assuaged the anguish in his heart and mind, softened the sorrow, and leavened the load of bitterness. Beth *had* been part of Ball's scheme, then. She *had* known what she was doing. For no other sensible reason would she have gone as far away as Independence, and farther, before she made a connection with travelers and headed right back toward this very country where her husband was hiding. It was a sordid, bitter revelation, a hard pill to swallow.

Will sat for a long time, sifting through the tangle of his life and eventually arriving at the unalterable, bare truth. It didn't make him feel any better, but in a sense he felt relief. The threads of each skein were worked out to their ends, and he could see each exactly as it was. For his dead wife there was a bridgeless pity. She had been beautiful, a vital girl to whom a weaker man would have given in to her continual plaints for the best things of life. Will had been a sobering counterbalance to her exuberance. They had gotten along well. Evidently Jim Ball was weak enough to turn to banditry for her. The results were certain and evident, like the retribution had been.

Will smoked a cigarette to its end, snuffed it out, and got back on the patient horse, gazing somberly into the east. There was just the faintest hint of light, and he knew dawn wasn't far off.

Striking over the ridge that separated him from the outlaw encampment with a recklessness that made rocks scurry under his horse's hoofs, he yanked out the carbine, sat clearly outlined for a moment looking down, then dismounted, led the horse out of harm's way, and picked out the dull black of the dead campfire.

The first shot ricocheted off a rock with an unearthly whine. The second brought the men up in a flurry of wildly abandoned pallets, and Will levered up the third shot but didn't squeeze it off. He watched the wild pandemonium below. Scraggly, unkempt wraiths ran blindly to their horses. Several only bridled their animals. Others cried out in alarm over the loss of two mounts, were handed up behind some who were mounted, and dust flew. It seemed like the camp was abandoned in less than a minute. No one threw lead at Will's ridge, where he watched out of lackluster eyes as the renegades broke out onto the desert floor in a mad scramble, then he lowered the carbine, and threw two fast ones in behind them. They swerved to a man and raced frantically ahead, in the general direction of Havasu.

The stillness engulfed Will as he returned to his horse, reloaded the carbine prudently, and swung up, reined down into the deserted camp, found two abandoned parfleches partly filled with jerky that he ate slowly while the horse drank and grazed. It was an hour later that rider and horse, refreshed, went back toward the Big Sink, over the trail the outlaws had used the day before, and Will saw the faintest pastels of dawn breaking over the rim of the dead expanse of land he had studied with such awe from the eminence of Pilot Rock as he swung down the trail, thankful for the chill of a new day.

The sun spilled its molten deadliness down the cringing land when Will was halfway across the desert, tracing with no effort the shuffling tracks left by the outlaws. His mind was in a sort of lethargy that allowed the vastness of the desert to go unnoticed, and even the heat bent off his back with a scourging he ignored. Hunger, more than anything but his thoughts, gouged into his spirit. The snack back at the outlaw camp had whetted an appetite previously ignored. With the sun throwing its full fury against him, he shot two quail by ground sluicing a covey, roasted, and ate them before he went on.

It was better than twenty-four hours later that an ugly, dark wart appeared on the horizon. Will's aching eyes held to the thing. He knew it was the far side of the desert at last. He watched it come toward him with aggravating slowness, assuming perspective, shape, and meaning. Thistleton.

The town was studied ugliness and sordid neglect to the gaunt, cold-eyed man who rode through its careless traffic on a scarecrow horse ready to drop. The livery barn loungers watched his approach in silence. Not many men dared the Big Sink in the middle of summer, and the few who did usually were haunted-looking desperadoes with two guns. This rider had only one. They stared at this spectacle of a desert wraith, for man and horse were silvered with the pale, grayish sheen that came gradually to sift down on travelers across the desert.

But more than anything else the grim, sober-faced citizens of Thistleton grew taciturn at the sight of the dull old badge he wore. The fact that he had come from the west made a difference, too. The Big Sink was no-man's land, an inhospitable, harsh world that belonged only to the desperate, kill-crazy, wanted prey from half the known world. Towns on both sides were the places where the stolen gold was accepted in greater amounts than anywhere along the frontier for supplies. Thistleton was no exception. Riches there came illegally. Citizens understood the need for law, but didn't like its presence just the same.

Will felt the quietness of the sluggish little desert-fringe town, chalked it up to the recent tragedy of the ravished freight train, and stabled his horse without lingering. He sought a café run by a slatternly, middle-aged woman, and ordered a large meal of meat and potatoes and coffee, black and lots of it.

The woman's hair was dowdy with neglect and hung carelessly over every plate of food she put on the wrought, slab counter. She eyed the gaunt, strange man with the sweaty clothes with no particular interest. Her voice was as whiningly garrulous as a rasp sliding over glass, when she spoke.

"Well, I expect the lynching brought you, too, eh, stranger?" She was eyeing the battered nickel badge with an accusing look.

Will's head came up slowly. His eyes felt like the lids were coated with fine emery paper underneath, against the eyeballs. "What lynching?" He said it very slowly, holding her in his glance and not bothering to raise his inflection to make a question of it.

133

"Hell, you *are* a stranger, ain't you? The lynching the boys pulled last night. That renegade they caught out by Boothill."

Will's weariness made him impatient. "All right . . . dammit . . . who got lynched?"

The woman's eyes read the mounting irritation plainly enough. She shrugged easily. "That feller named Ball. One of the *hombres* who waylaid the freight outfit and high-graded 'em."

Will looked at the woman for a long, hushed moment, then dropped his head listlessly to the plate. He ate without being completely conscious of what he was doing. The food left a thick coating of grease on the top of his mouth. Perversely enough, he remembered something Annalee had said once. He had given more than his life, when he went out to serve his country in what seemed so long ago, in the Mormon fiasco.

He finished the meal and made a cigarette. The woman filled his coffee cup again, blowing her hair out of her eyes with an abrupt, noisy gesture of a jutted lower lip and a quick expulsion of breath.

"Who hung him?"

"The boys," she said with a shrug. "I don't know. Didn't go down there. They hung him to the balk of the livery barn's front door. Man . . . you could hear the cussing and carrying-on half the night." Her watery eyes looked amusedly at him. " 'Twasn't outrage made 'em do, I don't think. Just that he might talk . . . or something. After all, the chore was done too close to Thistleton. Folks don't want the Army bustin' in here nosin' around. They're mad about them owlhooters makin' such a big stink right near town like that."

Will wasn't listening. He was hearing the Kid telling him again that Ball hadn't arrived until *after* the fight. It had been justice in a way, but Ball's brief, love-inspired flight into outlawry had been a series of blunders from start to finish, and in the end he had been lynched for something he might have even been riding hard to prevent, and certainly didn't participate in.

Will was still sitting there thinking, when the sheriff walked in. He saw the man coming down the duckboards through the dingy window and speculated on how fast news travels in a small town.

"Howdy, Deputy."

Will nodded silently at the ruddy-faced, heavily paunched man who eased down on the bench beside him. The final barb of his thoughts was that Beth, in her girlish, innocent way had driven Ball into outlawry, and he, because he was too weak— too much in love to protest—had gone out. Now both were dead, and by a sardonic twist of fate neither had died because of things they were more than passingly concerned with.

"What town you from?"

The words jarred Will back to the present. He looked at the perspiring, red face, found himself disliking the man's shifting eyes where a pattern of deceit moved in the background, and answered shortly.

"Havasu."

"That so? Well, we've heard you got some good boys over there. Make it plain unhealthful for lawbreakers around that country, the last few months. Just ride in?"

Will nodded, making another cigarette, smoking it, and looking out the doorless opening.

"Well . . . did you come for a purpose?"

Will turned slowly. The question made him almost smile when he thought back to the tortures he had endured to get to this tumor on the fringe of nowhere. "I reckon," he said laconically. "Sort of a poor time of the year for a pleasure ride."

The red face got redder. "Tell me, Sheriff, how come you let this man Ball get lynched?"

The coldness of the voice hit the sheriff where he lived. His eyes flashed in the thick, blunt setting of coarse features. "Listen, Deputy, Thistleton's just been the site of the biggest single attack by renegades on the frontier. Folks was damned riled. Now, I got two deputies and myself. We. . . ."

Will made a contemptuous gesture with his hand, then dropped the cigarette, and ground it out with a spur rowel. "Forget it. I don't reckon it'd make a difference to you, if you knew Jim Ball wasn't in on that attack . . . would it?"

"What do you mean? He told us. . . ."

"You were in on it, too, huh?" Will's blue eyes swung in a cold arc to the florid face. "Damned poor law you got here."

"Listen, you! We don't. . . ." The sheriff got up ponderously and was standing wide-legged, bracing into the calm scorn on Will's face.

"Oh, shut up." Will came tiredly off the bench, looking down into the heavier, shorter man's face. A writhing, anguished deadliness shone out of his eyes. "I talked to the man who led that attack. The Verde River Kid. He had absolutely nothing to gain by lying. He told me Ball didn't arrive until *after* the fight."

"But he said . . . just before they swung him up. . . ."

"What'd you expect him to say," Will spat out savagely, "when you had him at the end of a rope? You fool! Of course he'd say anything he had to, if he thought it'd take your rope off his neck. Told you who the others were, too, didn't he?"

"Yeah, I got the names. All of 'em."

"Sure you have." Will said it with scathing contempt, letting his eyes range downward over the thick-set torso with its obviously built-in brutality and licentiousness. "Sure you have. And they're the right names, too, more'n likely, because Ball knew who the Kid was riding with. All except the

one you hung . . . you fool!" The blue eyes were icy now.
"Thistleton's got a reputation for this sort of thing . . . and
other things as bad . . . along the frontier. I've heard a lot
about your town since I came to this end of the world, mister,
damned little was good, and now I can understand why.
Where'd you bury him?"

"Beside the woman. The one he was blubbering over when
we found him in the cemetery and knocked the truth out of
him."

It was absolutely the worst thing the sheriff could have
said under the circumstances, but he was sullenly raging inwardly now. Will's physical weariness had dropped away. It
was replaced by a mental sickness that seized him and bub-
bled in a pool of fury. He regarded the lawman for a full ten
seconds in silence, then he lashed out with a blow that spi-
raled up toward the other man's face and exploded in a claret
pinwheel of ruin that broke the sheriff's nose and stretched
him senseless on the floor.

The woman behind the counter didn't yell, but her
fiercely indrawn breath was half as loud as a scream would
have been. Will stared blankly, then stepped over the body,
and walked out of the café.

A man standing in the shade of a snooker-parlor overhang
told him where the cemetery was. He walked the full distance
to the far knoll beyond town and found the graves side by
side. The sky was becoming a darkened slate color that
robbed the sun of much of its head. Will didn't notice. He
read the headboards, then the tempest that had been pent-up
so long within him burst, and he passed out.

VI

The smell of rain was in the air, and a massive, brawny man in an undershirt and wearing a shiny old leather apron was standing over him, nudging him gently with a boot-toe, when he looked up. There was, strangely enough for the battered, hard features, an unaccustomed look of softness on the dented face.

"Come on, pardner," the big man said, "let's get back to town." The voice was gentle.

Will stood up. "Who're you?"

"Burt Savage. I'm a blacksmith in town. Also head of the new town council. You oughtn't to have busted Sheriff Lowndes like that." The steady gray eyes were thoughtful. "He tried to stop it, I'm pretty sure. It was one of those mob lynchings." The huge shoulders rose and fell. "You can't stop 'em. You know that."

"But . . . Ball wasn't in the fight at all."

"Maybe not, but he was one of 'em. Said so himself."

Will let it go. There was a certain uselessness in arguing against what he knew now was some inexplicable destiny that had dealt this hand out to Beth and her illegal husband.

"Listen, will you do something for . . . them? I'll pay whatever it costs. Will you hire a stonemason to make them . . . both . . . real nice headstones? With scrollwork, like they have back in the States, and . . . ?"

"Sure, pardner, sure. Forget it. Won't cost you a dime. I'll see that the city pays for it." The big man's glance was calm and level. "I'm a widower," he said simply. "It takes something like that to make a man see a lot of stuff in life other fellers don't see."

The massive bulk relaxed a little, the huge chest narrowed slightly, and the settling weight lowered and protruded around a waist that was beginning to thicken. This man was no longer young, although his face was smooth enough, in spite of its scars and dents.

"You want to take the kid back with you? They had folks somewhere, didn't they? The kid's got better'n she's likely to get coming to her."

Will was stunned. He had forgotten Beth's baby. Completely forgotten it. He stared for a startled, alarmed moment. The thought of a small baby was so foreign to his world it frightened him.

The blacksmith misinterpreted the astonishment. He wagged his head slowly. "Listen, pardner, you knew about them folks. I sort of feel like there's something we people in Thistleton don't know about. I'm not pryin' because I don't care, but . . . the kid's deserving. I'll make a trade with you. Thistleton'll take care of the graves, keep the weeds down, all such things as that, if you'll see that the baby gets to her kinsmen. Someday she'll want to come back and she'll find just a couple of well-tended gravestones when she does. You just give her the first hand along in life . . . back to her kinsfolk. That sound like a good trade, pardner?"

Will's tongue was doubled back against the very real hurt in his throat. That's what made the single word sound so harsh when he spoke and extended his hand. "Shake."

The blacksmith shook and flushed in masculine embarrassment, keeping his eyes on the entwined hands, then he looked up wryly. "That the hand that hit the sheriff? Well, you broke his nose and knocked out two teeth."

"I'm about half sorry, mister."

The smith chuckled in obvious relief. It was an infectious, melodious sound coming from the big chest and rippling into the lowering, darkening day. "I'm not," he said finally. "He's only got three months left of his term. Everybody makes mistakes. . . . Well, he won't be here next year, anyway. That's what the new council's trying to make up for . . . correct . . . things around Thistleton that've been sort of slip-shod for the past few years. It'll take a bit of doing, but we'll do it." He looked thoughtfully down at the two mounds. "Come on. We'll go back and get the kid. My sister's been keeping her. She's terrible fond of kids. Hers are grown and gone now. She'll more'n likely howl like a wounded eagle when I tell her you're taking the kid away. Sis is awful fond of kids."

They walked back toward town, and Will missed the only chance he'd ever have to side-step this new, frightening responsibility, and didn't even know it. If the smith's sister liked children so well, he could leave Beth's baby in Thistleton, but the idea didn't even occur to him.

The blacksmith was speaking again when they finally came to the end of the plank walk. "She's awful cute, too . . . dammit. Funny how them little tiny ones grow on a man, isn't it?"

He was looking at Will, so the lawman nodded and pried his tongue off the roof of his mouth. He was still appalled at this abrupt, unsuspected twist of strange fate. "Yeah, I reckon. Fact is, I don't know much about kids . . . babies."

The big man smiled. "Me neither, but it don't keep a man from liking 'em."

The next two hours were an ordeal he'd never forget. He made arrangements with some teamsters who were freighting out of Thistleton toward Havasu to drive the outlaw's saddle horse back across the desert with their loose stock. There was no alternative. With a baby on his hands stage travel was the only practical way of returning.

The blacksmith's sister proved to be a formidable woman nearly as burly as her brother, not only formidable physically, but in determination and intelligence as well. She stuffed the pocket of Will's new coat—one he'd bought to replace the filthy rag he'd worn out in the hunt for the Verde River Kid's gang—with unbleached pieces of muslin she called diapers, of which Will had less than passing knowledge, plus some prepared bottles of real cow's milk, and a tightly cramped, voluminous letter of instructions that he read and re-read as the stage rolled over the flat desert road, thinking that only the last, hastily written postscript was sensible at all. That was where the blacksmith's sister had finally decided, after studying him, that he wasn't capable of following her detailed instructions, anyway, and had told him frankly in her heavy scrawl to *hunt up a decent-looking woman on the way and do what she tells you.*

The little girl had Beth's pert nose and a little of her wide-eyed, naïve look around the eyes. She was reluctant to transfer her affections from the smith's sister to Will and wailed with prodigious resentment at the switch. But, by the time the stage pulled out, her tears had wrought a magic all their own. She slept as deeply and completely as anyone could, head lolling on Will's shoulder and her little warm body, light and strangely shapeless, a bundle of trust against his chest.

He watched the barren world of desert sweep past and rocked gently with the motion of the coach. There were two other passengers, an obvious drummer from the States and a woman of ample proportions who might have been a merchant's wife or a soldier's mother. She had a hard time keeping her eyes from Will's face. She would glance briefly, skimmingly, out at the lowering beauty around them, then swing back, and look again.

The smell of rain still hung in the air. It had poured stingily during the night on the desert, but Will hadn't known it until they were over the gray land where the dust had been settled and the air had a metallic clearness to it. It made him feel refreshed.

The baby brought his mind back to the present when she awakened, gave a long, jerky sigh, and began to twist immediately, making small, disgruntled, animal sounds. Will glanced at her in wonder, sensing the discomfort and guessing it was the stage that made her that way. It wasn't.

A short, rich laugh floated briefly through the coach before it was whipped away in the warm air. Will looked up. The woman traveler was watching his helplessness mount with each turn of the wheels. He grinned embarrassedly at her and shrugged his shoulders eloquently, saying nothing. The woman bent a little, her amber eyes laughing up into his.

"You aren't used to babies, are you?"

"No, ma'am," he said honestly, recalling the postscript on the lengthy and intricate letter of instructions the blacksmith's sister had forced on him between scowls and looks of great anxiety.

"They sleep a lot when they're contented," she said tentatively, looking into the little face that was getting redder by the minute.

Will followed the woman's glance to the child in his lap. He shook his head. "Well . . . maybe," he said dryly, "but this one doesn't."

"Maybe I could help."

Will looked up quickly. The relief on his face was almost ludicrous. Here was a female, and, to his mind, this baby had already formed an affinity—perhaps even some kind of a child's secret alliance—with all women, race and age not-withstanding.

The woman held out her hands. "May I hold her?"

Will glanced at her hands, recalling the blacksmith's sister's repeated admonitions about cleanliness around babies.

A wide, knowing smile flashed at him almost mischievously. "Oh, don't worry," she said, "they're clean."

He handed the squirming bundle across the coach and saw the drummer's interest in the transaction out of the corner of his eye. The child went willingly enough, still annoyed about something but less angry than before. Will nodded. His suspicions about little baby girls and some mysterious understanding they had with womankind solidified. The woman's voice jarred him out of his relief.

"Those rags you have in your coat pocket. Give me one, will you?"

Dutifully he complied, watched somewhat in horror and embarrassment as the woman bent low, hands plying an almost instinctive ritual with all women, and the diapers were changed. The twinkling eyes looked up triumphantly, slyly, at him.

"Now . . . what have you to feed her?"

Will fished for one of the bottles he'd received back in Thistleton and held it out quickly and looked on in surprise as the woman took up a parasol, leaned far out, and jabbed insistently at the driver's leg where it dangled over the side of the boot. It took four lunges and three direct hits before the stage slowed to a dusty halt, and the guard came around one side, shotgun at the ready, and the driver appeared on the opposite side.

The woman flashed them both a magnificent smile, passed the baby to the astonished driver whose mouth closed over annoyed words of near profanity as though he'd been struck in the stomach, and whose tufted, stormy eyebrows shot upwards in something akin to supplication as the woman stepped down, went past him, and stopped to gather fagots.

Will divined the purpose readily enough, got down, and helped her. They had a small fire of dead brush twigs and buffalo chips going before the heavily armed guard came over wonderingly after a short talk with the drummer and watched, frozen-faced.

The driver hunkered by the little fire, watching the woman heat the bottle. He held the baby awkwardly, in discomfort, shaking his head at its smallness. "Make us late to Havasu," was all he could think to say.

The woman's eyes lifted challengingly, but her voice was as sweetly modulated as ever. "Do you mind, awfully?"

The tiny hands were gripping his massive, dirty, bronzed fingers, and squeezing them. He looked down, saw the uncontrolled, helpless little movements of the tiny body, and shook his head. "No," he said ponderously. "I reckon not." Raising narrowed, bleached-out eyes to the ferocious-looking guard he jerked his head at the man. "Ever notice how damned small their hands are, Jack? Looka there. Them fingernails. My Gawd, how'd you reckon anybody could make anything so damned little and have it turn out right?"

The guard bent down, studied the fingernails and puffy, dimpled little hands in general with all the grave attention of a scientist, then rocked back on his heels again thoughtfully. "Never noticed that before," he said sententiously, then, fearful lest he lost caste in this drama in the dead world of the Big Sink beside the little fire, he nodded expansively. "Oh . . . I've seen babies before, plenty of 'em." He bent forward again to see if she'd grasp his finger like she had the driver's. "But not this close up. I seen a woman chew up some porridge once, spit it into a tin cup, and spoon it into her kid." He raised his bearded, villainous face and looked at the woman by the fire. "That what you're fixin' to do, ma'am?"

The woman smiled and shook her head. "No, this is milk. It has to be warmed to about body temperature. She'll suck the rag stuffed in the end of the bottle."

The guard considered this somberly. "Seems like a terrible slow way to get a drink . . . don't it?"

The driver handed the baby to Will. "Yeah, it does. She'll get the milk out of the rag, and I expect it'll give her something to do, a-suckin' on it like that. Sort of pacify her, won't it?"

The woman stood up, shook the dust out of her skirt, and held out her arms for the baby. "That's about it," she said. "Now we can go on, if you wish."

The driver was surprised and showed it. "Hell, lady, you warmed the milk. Why'n't you give it to her?"

"I will, but she'll drink it better when the stage's rocking again. Sleep afterward, too."

"Oh," the driver said, mollified, suddenly past the act that he'd thought a form of cruelty before. To heat the milk and not give it to the baby, after all. Sort of like riding a thirsty horse across a creek and not letting him drink.

The guard leaned heavily on his shotgun barrel, watching with keen interest as the little girl relaxed all at once and all over, nuzzling the bottle with strange, unmannerly sounds that ranged from the echo of a cow pulling its foot out of the mud to the distant and frequent sounds of gunshots. He smiled, enthralled, showing a dazzling set of teeth through his beard.

"That beats hell," he said. "Don't it, Jeb?"

The driver nodded, too, still making no move to remount his box. "Yeah, it does for a fact. What'll they think of next?"

Will stomped out the little fire, kicked sand over it, and

looked at the adults. It opened his eyes to a side of human nature he'd never seen before. Almost smiling, he went over close to the woman and looked down. The baby was oblivious to everything but the bottle, eyes half closed, arms and legs, small beyond belief, dimpled and fat, too, dangling listlessly. The woman looked up at him, smiled, and held out the baby.

"Here. She's yours. You do it."

Will took the limp, warm bundle, heard the annoyed grunts that came from it at the transfer, held her like the woman had been doing, and felt a sudden, inexplicable surge of awe and triumph because the baby didn't object to his holding her. He looked across at the guard and driver. "We'd better roll, boys. Havasu'll think we been ambushed . . . or something."

"Yeah," the driver said slowly, still absorbed. "I reckon so."

They pulled out again, the land slipping past slowly at first, until momentum had been gained, then whipping by in a cool, leaden, ominous panorama of moist desert, a little sticky with former heat that was gentled now in its inferno, until the sameness of the motion rocked a very small girl to sleep, still unwilling to give up the nearly empty bottle and holding the rag in her mouth.

Will looked across at the woman. She wasn't looking at him any more. Her eyes were riding across the changing landscape, unseeing, sober and reflective. "Thank you, ma'am."

The eyes came around to him, looked squarely into his for a moment, then the head inclined a little, the lips raised in a near smile, and she spoke. "You're welcome." It was an acknowledgement with an overtone of haunting unhappiness. Will watched the face turn a little again, so the eyes could lose themselves out over the desert, and felt a thin lacing of sorrow having come with them in the old coach.

146

★ ★ ★ ★ ★

Havasu hadn't had any rain. The sun was as mercilessly supreme as it had been when he had left with Clem Everest. Somewhere, out on the desert, the parched earth had sucked the vital juice out of the rain clouds.

The town sweated under its stingy cottonwood shade, and the sound of dogs and small boys came perpetually from the sluggish, shallow stream that lay east of town. Will heard the stage wheels grind into inches-thick dust, the rims and tires snarling in contact with the plank walk, then the motion ceased, and he was home.

He stayed back, letting the woman descend ahead of him, then behind the drummer before he climbed out. The blue eyes flashed over the usual, thin crowd of hangers-on who always gathered when a stage was due, loafers, idling cowboys, and ranch folk in town for a day, but aside from the mildly curious, slightly familiar faces, there was no one on hand he wanted to see.

Shifting the sleeping baby's bulk, he watched the slow surprise, almost consternation, jump into the faces that were turned his way. The desire to laugh aloud at the obvious thoughts in the startled eyes was strong, but he didn't alter expression.

Will Brennan, the notorious bounty hunter, had returned with, of *all* things, a baby! He could imagine it going from mouth to mouth through the Havasu country, like the whisper of a brush fire. He turned away, toward his room over the Federal Eagle, with a tight, sardonic smile.

Stan Tracy looked up in surprise when Will walked in. He had heard the talk about Will Brennan's returning from the hunt with a small baby. Will ranged along the bar until he came to his customary place and nodded at Stan. The barman went over, nodded slightly, and spoke first.

"Where's the kid, Will?"

Will smiled thinly. "Havasu's got a good ear, Stan," he said dryly. "She's upstairs. I put her on my bed and banked a bunch of stuff around her so's she won't roll off." He shook his head wryly. "When they aren't asleep, they're sure active." The blue eyes flickered over the barman's blank features with new interest. "You ever have one, Stan?"

The look of shock and horror he got were better than the answer he didn't get. Stan Tracy's face settled into mild reproach finally. All he said was: "Bran mash, Will?"

Will shook his head. "No, where can I hire a woman to take care of her?"

The barman batted his eyes owlishly, regarding Will oddly, then frowned in thought. In his trade questions were routine, like their answers, but this was one he'd never been asked before.

"Well . . . there's Beulow Wilson's wife. The woman that does the wash, I mean."

Will vetoed the suggestion with a curt shake of his head. "You don't understand, Stan. This is a little girl. They've got to be handled different from little boys. Woman's got to have clean hands . . . and all. I want a lady who. . . ."

"Yeah, I reckon that's right, too." Stan bent his head lower, concentrating. "How about Arch Means's wife? She's got four of her own." The sloping, fleshy shoulders rose and fell slightly, apologetically. " 'Course, they're always kind of filthy-looking, but they seem healthy."

Will shook his head again. His answer was pained and exasperated. "Stan, I told you. *This* is a little *girl!*"

"Yeah . . . yeah." The sound of the barman's breathing was broken in the cool silence by the sound of a frantic, blue-tailed fly that had blundered stupidly into a spider's web, and also by the muted drone of some old men at the blackjack table in a far corner.

"I got it, Will . . . Sheriff Dexter's wife. Maude's raised six. They're all gone now, married and what not, but she raised every last one of them." The hopeful glint in Tracy's eyes replaced the forlorn, unpleasant look he'd worn toward Will since the manhunter had captured his brother. "How about her?"

Will regarded the barman stonily for a silent moment, then nodded. "That's it, Stan. Thanks." He turned on his heel.

"Hey! Wait a second. Don't you want your bran mash? I'll whip one up on the house."

The manhunter turned back with a rueful smile. "No thanks, Stan. Later, maybe."

He was halfway across the sawdusted floor, heading for the batwing doors, when Tracy's glance lifted, lost its surprised look, and clung to his back with an agreeable little grin spreading out over the usually blank features.

Clem Everest saw Will coming down the duckboards, his dusty coat flopping awkwardly around the bulge of his gun. Clem was about to enter the sheriff's office, hesitated, and nodded as Will came up.

"Man, you were born lucky."

"Why?"

"That Verde River Kid's got eleven thousand in gold on his mangy hide."

"The hell you say."

Clem shoved the door open and stepped aside for Will to enter. "Yeah. He's wanted from here to Texas."

"How about the buckskin horse? Did he bring in his load, too?"

The deputy's eyes widened in sudden recollection. "Yeah, but good Lord, man, you dang' near killed that 'breed. The shift was changing at the livery barn when the critter came in. No one knew what to do. Whether to risk cutting the *hombre* loose or routing out the sheriff. By the time they'd got their minds made up, that Murphy feller was about strangled." Clem wagged his head in disapproval. "That's going a little hard on 'em, Will, ain't it?"

Will shrugged. "I didn't think so, not after the way he pulled that knife on me. Any reward on him, Clem?"

"Couldn't find any."

They entered the office, and Sheriff Dexter looked up from his table, squinted a tentative smile, and interrupted their talk. "It was like shooting fish in a rain barrel. They was so darned used up . . . them and their horses . . . about all we had to do was haul up in front of 'em with the posse, and they give up right there."

Clem smiled dourly. "And, as usual, the Army come along ten hours behind schedule and took 'em off our hands." He let the smile fade. "But, you never told me what you were up to. We was about to strike out with a posse and hunt for your remains."

Will looked down at his hand. "Yeah, well . . . I'm sorry. I had a little unfinished business over at Thistleton."

Tim Dexter kept a steady glance on the manhunter, waiting, but Will said no more. He grunted then, and lowered his shaggy old eyebrows.

Will looked over at him. "Tim, I got a favor to ask of you . . . I . . . got a baby." He saw the abrupt stiffening, the clear, jolting astonishment in Dexter's face.

Everest's half-made cigarette jerked suddenly, tearing the paper. "Damn!" the big deputy said, shocked.

Will laughed aloud at them. It was a rusty sound. "No, it

isn't mine." He felt uncomfortable and disloyal as soon as he'd said it. "I'll take that back. It's half mine." The looks he got made it clear that he was only adding to the bewilderment. "Well," he said desperately, "I got this baby. She's mine, too, but not like you *hombres* are thinking."

Everest completed the new cigarette, inhaled, and threw a glinting, skeptical look at Will. "There just ain't any other way . . . that *I* know of, Will," he said laconically, drawlingly.

Will's face was russet color. "I got her boys. She's the littlest thing you ever saw. By Gawd, I swear she feels like she's got no bones in her body." Dexter's awry look persisted. He hadn't moved since Will originally spoke of the baby. "Tim, your wife raised six of 'em, didn't she?" The sheriff didn't nod or answer. Will was perspiring like a racehorse. I'll pay her whatever she asks, Tim, if she'll just take this baby . . . my baby . . . and sort of mother it . . . for a while."

He suddenly went dumb. An awful, tremendous thought had just occurred to him. What was he going to do with a baby? He had to raise it. It was his. Half his, anyway. Beth's baby. He knew nothing about babies, had no home or occupation that would allow him to raise it, and this was just the beginning. Babies grew into people, he knew vaguely, but it took an awfully long time, and in the meantime someone had to guide them, educate them, clothe and feed them. It was a crushing responsibility. The more he thought of it, the worse it seemed.

Sheriff Dexter's voice was striving to reach through the shock that gripped him. "Married, too. All but Alfred. Al's an Arizona Ranger. He ain't married yet, but Tim . . . he's the youngest . . . he's married now. Happened last spring. They live near San Carlos. Maude's the best mother I ever saw. Not just because she's my wife, either." Dexter snorted disdainfully. "A man lives with a woman thirty years, and she don't fool him any." He paused, thinking, then looked up shrewdly. "I tell you what you do, Will. Where is this kid?"

"In my room."

"Well, go get him and. . . ."

"It's a her, Tim."

Dexter shook his head briefly. "At this age it makes no difference, believe me, I know. You go get her and take her down to my house. Just knock on the door and hand her to Maude and tell her I said you need someone to mother the kid for a while."

Will had very large doubts. "You reckon she'd do it, Tim?"

Dexter's eyes were squinted with slow humor. "Oh, she'll do it all right, Will. But you got to be braced for what she'll tell *you*, too."

"What do you mean?"

Dexter shrugged. "Darned if I rightly know, only that most folks in town know you're a single man, Will." He cleared his throat noisily. "Enough said on that score. Anyway, you take a woman Maude's age and hand 'em something they're tickled as hell over, and eight out of ten of 'em'll just up and rip into you with a first-class tongue lashing. Don't ask me why, boys, I don't know. I just know they will, that's all."

Will arose slowly, not altogether convinced of the wisdom of the action. "Well, Tim, I got the bounty coming on the Verde River Kid. I'll tell her I'll make it over to her if she'll sort of figure out what the baby ought to have."

Dexter blew his nose into a blue handkerchief with immense cabbage roses printed on it and shook his head. "Well, I don't expect I'd do that just yet, Will. Don't talk about giving women money the same time you hand 'em a baby. Just let me handle that end of it when I get home."

Will nodded, feeling inferior for the first time, to the small, wizened old man behind the littered table. "All right, Tim. I'll do it like you say. Hope we don't both land in the hot water up to our necks." He turned to the deputy. "You want to come with me, Clem? Ever see a little baby up close?"

Everest looked startled. He smoked for a second in thought, then shrugged, and stood up. "No, can't say that I have. Sure, I'll go."

Sheriff Dexter waited until his two deputies had gone, the sound of their spurs ringing small behind the closed door of his office, then he emitted a loud, gasping sigh and shoved out of the chair, went to the safe, fished among its unkempt contents until he found a bottle of rye whisky, uncorked it, and took two big swallows, replaced the bottle, and leaned on the safe, gasping and swearing in a weak, incredulous tone of voice.

Will heard the racket before he got the door unlocked. Clem was looking worried. He went over to the side of the bed and looked down at the small red and furious face. The baby's anger was apparent even to him. He shook his head in awe.

"Will, she's got a hell of a temper."

For a second Will longed for the woman on the stage, then he had an inspiration. Running a hand under her, he felt the copious dampness, thumbed his hat to the back of his head, looked around until he saw the pile of diapers he had taken from his coat pocket on the bureau, selected one gingerly, folded it as his memory dictated, went back to the bed, and, flushing scarlet, went to work. Clem looked on in rapt amazement, noting each awkward movement of the bounty hunter with admiration.

"Well, hell!" the tall deputy said when the howls had di-

153

minished to small, spasmodic sounds of garrulousness. "You mean she was raising all that Cain over being damp?"

Will nodded in a superior way. "Yeah, they don't like wet pants." He lifted the baby and held her out. "Here . . . you hold her while I gather up her stuff."

Clem backed away two long steps. "Oh, no, *hombre*. Listen, she looks like she'd bite a man."

Will frowned. Small hands clutched at him. He brought her in close to his unshaved cheeks. Tiny spasms still shook her, and little wet sounds came out of the perspiring face. Will felt a crazy, compassionate sensation in his chest and throat. He stood perfectly still, letting the mood hold him in its peculiar thrill, then he motioned with his head toward the dresser.

"Get one of those rags, Clem. Wipe her face, will you?"

Everest moved reluctantly, almost grimly, reached around cautiously, and mopped at the tiny fairy pearls on her upper lip. Will twisted his head as far as he could, watched critically, and spoke again.

"Nose, too, Clem. She sounds like a wind-broke horse."

Clem, emboldened, did a thorough job, then stepped back with a small grin of inspection, and regarded his handiwork carefully. Will wanted to laugh. The tall deputy's face was ludicrous. "All right, fetch those traps on the bureau. Those bottles and the rags . . . diapers . . . and let's go."

They went down the rickety stairway and out into the sun blast of the scorched roadway. Havasu was treated to as novel a sight as its sanguine old street had ever seen. Will Brennan, the embittered, cold, unfriendly, ruthless manhunter, stalking up the plank walk with a bold, challenging look at those who stared, and lean Deputy Sheriff Clem Everest trailing along, red-faced, gripping a disheveled bundle of diapers in one hand and several bottles of milk with rags dangling from their open ends in the other hand. If anyone laughed, Will and Clem, sensitive enough to hear it, would know it, but strangely no one did laugh, really; some smiled slyly, but most of the watchers, idlers and shoppers, just stared. The little girl had ash-blonde hair and rosy cheeks that were flushed against the dark cloth of Will's coat.

The look of the two hard-eyed deputies, burned bronze and heavily armed, was incongruous in a way, but the little girl wasn't, and the frontiersmen saw her more than the men, anyway. They didn't laugh, hardly at all.

VII

Maude Dexter was aghast. For a moment she was speechless, then the torrent descended exactly as the sheriff had said it would. Clem was appalled. He stood back, watching the baby go into large, capable hands without awakening, and surreptitiously deposited his burden on a sofa and ducked back out onto the porch, content to wait out there for Will.

"What," demanded the gray-haired woman, "is a man like *you* doing with a child like *this?*"

Will was shaken. "She's mine," he said defensively.

Maude Dexter sat down and cradled the baby in an ample lap. Her blue eyes never wavered from a careful scrutiny of the child. She didn't even look up when she spoke again. "She's a beautiful little doll, Brennan. Just beautiful." A lacing of awe was in the older woman's voice. "Where ever did you get her, man?" Maude Dexter looked up, saw Will's expression, and rushed on. "*Pshaw!* You men and your code of ethics. No questions, no answers. Big, strong, silent men with guns. *Humph!* Dunces . . . that's what you are, every blessed last one of you. Dunces! About as smart as

155

wood ticks. Now you tell me, Brennan, where you got this child?"

There was more, lots more, so much more in fact that Will never could recall it all, and none of it had been complimentary up to this point. Scathing, scornful, and vehement—and embarrassing, too—but unanswerable. Will shifted his weight, moved his hat from one fist to the other, and looked down at the baby. It took a long time to get over the sting, but when he finally did, he felt a peculiar kinship with the gray-headed, intently blue-eyed woman with the matronly lines and honest, outspoken mouth. He told her the story from the very beginning. It was a rambling, silence-studded narrative that hurt to tell. It came out almost incoherently in places, too, because he'd never spoken to another living soul about all of it before, and each acid memory brought up another, equally bitter. But he never once mentioned Annalee. Just the story of himself and Beth, and the outlaw, Ball, and their baby.

Maude Dexter said nothing for several minutes. She rocked gently, looking down at the little girl. When she did speak, the spark of excitement had died out of her voice. It was soft with her memories of past hurts, too, and she didn't look up at Will when she spoke.

"All right, you go back and tell Tim to come home now. I'll need him this afternoon. Tell him to stop at O'Brien's and get a big jar of sweet oil and . . . and . . . some unbleached cloth. Now . . . go along, Brennan."

Will went back outside, saw the wondering glance Clem shot at him as they clumped back toward town, and shrugged his relief. "Damn, Clem . . . ," he said, and let it die right there.

Everest walked along, head down, for a while. In fact, they were in front of the sheriff's office before he stopped, looked up, and spoke. "Will, by God, they're sure made fine, aren't they?"

"Babies?"

"Yeah. It'd almost be worth getting married and taking to raising cattle to have a few of 'em, wouldn't it?"

Will considered this for a space before he spoke, then he scratched the back of his neck doubtfully. "Darned if I know, Clem. By golly, a man's got to take an awful lot when he gets one. Then . . . you think it through, you've got an awful responsibility. They got to be watched over and fed and clothed . . . and all . . . too." He squinted at Clem's very grave- looking face and thought of Beth's baby asleep in Maude Dexter's lap. "But . . . by Gawd, Clem, you're right, right as rain, boy. They're sure made fine, too, aren't they?"

Clem nodded, pushed on ahead, swung in through the office door, and slumped on the wall bench again. Will sat down next to him and regarded the sheriff somberly.

"Your wife says for you to get right home and get some sweet oil and unbleached cloth at O'Brien's store, on the way."

Dexter got up with a wavering, questioning smile. "See? What'd I tell you? Maude'll take over. You can't beat 'em in a fix like this."

"I don't know," Clem said slowly. "A man might want to, the way they cuss him out. Man! They sure get excited and sore, don't they?"

Dexter shrugged. "You would, too, if someone upped and handed you a baby . . . wouldn't you?"

Clem didn't answer. He didn't have to. Will and the sheriff both laughed out loud at the stricken look of congealed horror that showed in his eyes.

Dexter pushed a limp paper at Will. "Here. This is the reward paper on the Verde River Kid. You sign it like always, and we'll send it in." He took his hat up, grinned maliciously at the still ashen-faced Clem, and went out into the raging heat of the day.

Will went over to the table, picked up the reward claimer, read it, and signed it. He mentally calculated the amount of money he had made since coming to the Havasu country and becoming a deputy sheriff—a bounty hunter. It was considerable. Far more than he had when he had started his ranch back at Cottonwood. There was a degree of comfort in the feeling of modest wealth. He made a cigarette, smoked it slowly, and looked at Everest.

"Clem, I'll buy you a supper."

Everest smiled with his nod. "Best thing I've heard today." He got up, brushed self-consciously at his clothes, and turned toward the door at the same time it swung inward abruptly and Ellie Burch stood framed in the opening, looking past him at Will. Clem stood motionless in his tracks. He had seen Havasu's beauties, which were exceedingly rare and mostly married. None could hold a candle to the disturbing, tantalizing beauty of the black-haired girl in the doorway.

Will could feel his defenses coming up, and he was embarrassed as well. He looked down, without speaking, to Ellie, dropped and stepped on his cigarette, then raised his eyes again. The girl didn't notice the coolness, or, if she did, which was far more likely, she ignored it. Ellie was far too vital to be hampered by conventions, written, spoken, or just felt. She came into the room, closed the door, and leaned on it, half smiling at Will and completely ignoring Clem.

"Well? You got what you went after, I've heard."

Will looked out from under lowered lashes without moving his head. "What's the double meaning, Ellie?"

She pushed herself away from the door and walked over to him. "The Verde River Kid."

158

"Oh," he said with vast relief, then he shrugged. "I really didn't do much. Clem here brought him in."

"I know. You didn't come back with the posse, either. Where were you, Will?"

The uneasiness returned. "What's the difference? I just came along later."

She tossed her head in mild annoyance. "I don't want to talk here. Come on over to my room."

He shook his head. "I'm sorry, Ellie. Clem and I are going to supper."

She didn't look cut at all. "Good, come up after supper."

Will didn't speak. She searched his face for a moment, then crossed the room to the door, opened it, and nodded, still ignoring Clem, to the deputy's huge discomfort, and disappeared.

Clem let a long, sibilant sound come out of him. "Lord! *Who* was that?"

"It doesn't matter," Will said flatly. "Let's go eat."

It was a good effort but not good enough. Finally, in the midst of their late coffee, Clem asked about Ellie. Will sketched a very brief and brutal outline of her. Clem was silent after listening, stirring his coffee absently. Eventually he nodded toward Will and spoke.

"Well, for hell's sake, man. If a woman like *that* would throw herself at me like she did at you, I'd be willing."

Will got up, dumped enough silver for both meals on the counter, and turned away from Clem who was downing his coffee. "I'm going to look in on the kid, Clem. See you around town later, maybe."

Clem nodded absently, obviously listening without really hearing, and arose, too. Will left the café, walked through the blazing, late afternoon sunlight toward the Dexter's residence at the far southern end of Havasu, and grappled with

159

the half forgotten fear he had of Ellie Burch.

Tim Dexter greeted his deputy with a harassed look and a wag of his head. "Lord Almighty," he said. "You'd think this was the first one she ever handled. Come in."

Will followed the sheriff into the parlor, nodded to Maude Dexter where she threw him a glance from her rocker, and looked at the baby. It was lying in a swathing of painfully clean blankets on the floor, playing contentedly, making small, pleasant sounds. The wide blue eyes took in the bronzed man with the hat in his hands staring down at her, and she didn't move. Not even after Will knelt and hesitantly pushed a finger toward her. She reached out after a bit and felt for the digit, grasped it, pulled and pushed, then released it with a small baby's smile of trust. The expression looked more to Will like a grimace of great suffering.

"Maude's been asking me what her name is, Will."

The bounty hunter looked up, saw them both regarding him solemnly, and got stiffly to his feet. "I . . . don't know." He tried to remember if he had ever heard the baby's name mentioned and decided he hadn't.

It was apparent to Will, looking at the Dexters, that Maude had told his story to the sheriff. He shifted his feet uncomfortably. The spurs made a small, soft, musical sound. The baby turned its head quickly to seek the source of this pleasant sound.

Tim Dexter was looking at the child when he spoke. "Well, you could call her after her mother."

Will held his hat loosely at his side. The knuckles were showing white. "I reckon," he said. "We'll see, later. Tim, did you speak to Missus Dexter about . . . ?"

The sheriff looked strained. "Plenty of time, boy, plenty of time for that. Now, I reckon, she'd better go to bed, hadn't she, Maude?"

Will said good evening and left. The shadows were growing a little long before the west side of town. He went back to the Federal Eagle, hesitated, then pushed past, turned in, and went up the rickety stairs, down the hall, and knocked on the Burch girls' door. Ellie opened it, smiled brilliantly up at him, and stepped aside. Will entered, swinging his hat again, and looked past the older girl for Annalee. She wasn't there.

"I rather thought you'd come, Will."

He heard the mocking triumph in her voice, behind its attempted banter. "Where's Annalee?"

"Why? What difference does it make?" She closed the door and deliberately went up close to him.

He stepped back with a small, uneasy look. "Because . . . I want to ask her something."

"I'll answer it. What is it?"

"What is Beth's baby's name?"

Ellie looked startled. "That's an odd one. I didn't think you'd ask anything. . . ."

"Where's Annalee, Ellie?"

The black eyes were dazzlingly bright and alive again in an instant. She tossed her head a little and reached for him. "I don't remember the child's name. Beth was Annalee's friend, not mine."

Will stepped back a little, breaking the sudden hold she had taken of his upper arms. "That's why I want to see Annalee. Where the devil is she?"

Ellie's fingers were working along his arms so that he felt the pain from her fingernails. "She's gone back to Cottonwood . . . Will Brennan! . . . where you told her to go."

Will was stunned. A great uneasiness opened up in him. "Hell," he swore in surprise and disappointment. "I didn't tell *her* to go. I said for both of you. . . ."

"Forget it. That's water under the bridge. She's gone, and

you sent her. I'm still here and intend to stay . . . because you're here." She threw herself against him, reaching for his mouth. Will caught the scent of the perfume she wore. It reminded him of her sister, then his head was suddenly encircled and pulled down savagely until the soft warmth of her full-lipped mouth was beneath him. To Will, it was something that made his blood race like fire, but his own innate dislike of her kept him from responding enough even to put his arms around her.

Her lips were moving under his when he wrenched away, scorn and confusion vying for control of his glare. "Ellie, you're a fool. If I liked you well enough to do this voluntarily, don't you think I'd let you know?"

Dark blood mantled into her face under the satiny, cream-colored skin. "*You're* the fool, Will, not me. What have you left from Beth? What will Annalee ever give you? I'm a woman, at least. If you turn away from me, you'll. . . ."

"Regret it," he finished for her. "Well, then, I'll just have to regret it, Ellie." His eyes and tone, both, were wryly sarcastic.

She stared after him, seeing him cross the room, open the door without glancing back, and slam it behind him. He went down the gloomy hallway to the stairway without raising his eyes, went down the stairs and back out into the cool of early evening. Not until then did he draw a long breath and let it out slowly. The sound was ragged. He stood motionless for a long time, thinking, then he started off again.

Before he found Clem Everest again, the evening shadows had lengthened into solid darkness. Clem was in the card room of the Federal Eagle. Will nudged him and walked away. Clem looked up irritably, saw, read, and interpreted, and followed, careful to carry his cards with him.

"What's up, Will? You look like a mule just kicked you."

"Listen, Clem. I'm going to be gone for a week or so. Tell Tim for me, will you?"

Everest nodded his head up and down, looking his astonishment. Words were formed on his lips, but he didn't allow them to come out.

Will avoided the look of his friend. "I've got to go back where I came from. Maybe it won't take long. Maybe it will. I don't know. Wish I did," he added wryly. "Anyway, tell Tim to watch my kid, will you, Clem?"

"Sure," Clem said, mystified and sympathetic. He had come to like Will Brennan in the last few weeks more than he had ever thought he would before. Like the sheriff, Clem was conscious of a change, gradual and pervasive, that he liked and approved of in the manhunter. "Sure, pardner. Forget the kid. I'll see about her myself, every now and then. Look in on her every chance I get. Anyway, with Maude Dexter taking care of her, you got no worries. She'll do a better job than you could ever do . . . me, either."

"I know, Clem." The blue eyes came up quickly, a little abashed. Will extended his hand. *"Adiós, hombre."*

Clem shook the hand. "Well . . . hell! When you leaving?"

"Right now. The stage's at the barn, getting a switch of horses. I saw it pull in. I got to run. S'long."

"S'long." Clem still held his empty hand out, looking after Will. The louvered doors swung once, then vibrated gently on their oiled spindles, and Clem was standing alone. A disgruntled voice rose over the sounds in the subdued, murky room, and Clem turned slowly. One of the players was looking bellicosely at him, motioning with a beefy arm. "Come on, damn it, let's play, if we're going to." Clem walked back slowly. Some of Will Brennan's uncertainty had rubbed off on him.

The driver eased back on the seat, kicked out at the high hand brake, and raised the lines with a careless, easy flick. "*You,* there!" he roared, and the profanity that followed was singsong and without meaning, the badge of his calling passed down to all stage drivers from the old bull-team men whose monotonous lives made the erecting of fabulous oaths a thing of great pride and hair-curling ingenuity.

The horses leaned into their harnesses. Will felt the rocking lurch, then the quiet sound of big wheels with steel tires turning on freshly greased axles, and the pall of Havasu's shadow world began to roll past as the stage spun out of town, south, then turned east at the forks, and continued to rocket along in the evening.

Will was the only passenger until they stopped at Westport, a big Army camp. Two elderly ladies came aboard there with luggage that made both the guard and driver growl evilly under their breaths, then they went on. The women were transferred officers' wives returning East. Their conversation was vitriolic and uncomplimentary about the frontier. Will listened with small boredom until the constant mumbles overcame him. Anything, almost, was better than being alone in the seclusion of his own thoughts . . . almost. But he found in this instance his own cares were preferable.

Just closing his eyes against the whipping breeze that dashed its backlash from the coach into his face brought all the anxieties back in full force. The baby, she was his responsibility. Beth's father . . . her only living relative . . . had died shortly before he entered the Army. If Ball had relatives, he neither knew of them nor cared who, and where, they were, nor had he any intention of looking too closely. Beth's girl would be raised the way she should be raised, like a lady. His jaw unconsciously set over that.

The embarrassment he had felt at the Dexters' house

crowded in then, and he thought again of Annalee. Surely *she* would know the baby's name. Maybe, too, like she had said, she would know a whale of a lot more than he had thought she did.

The memory of Annalee's very serious, pained expression when she had told him brought a whimsical little smile to his face. He almost laughed. Well, maybe she did at that. He hoped she did, anyway, hoped with all his heart and soul she did, because that was why he was going back to Cottonwood, and, if she knew all she *ought* to know, why then his job would be immeasurably easier. He wanted to find out if Annalee knew something that had become crystal clear to him in the last fifty hours or so—that Will Brennan wanted her, needed her more than anything else on earth, that he was in love with her and had been, scarcely understanding it himself, since the day he had kissed her before he rode out with Clem Everest after the Verde River Kid's wolf pack.

At Indian Wells, which was nothing more than a stage station and blacksmith shop with hostler's hovels clustered in the shade of ancient trees, they stopped for a wheel greasing and another change of horses. Will went into the makeshift café there and drank two cups of coffee. A lean, dissipated-looking man no older in years than he was himself, but far more aged in general appearance and physique, sat frozen to his bench, staring. Will saw the look, recognized the face from years back, and ignored it. The man got up, crossed the room, and sank down beside Will.

"Mister, I'll bet my last dollar you're a fellow I knew four, five years ago."

"That so?" Will said coolly.

"Yeah, *hombre* named Brennan. Went out to Utah with Johnson's army during the Mormon troubles there."

Will turned with an unpleasant stare. "That's who I am,

Beacon. Now what do you want?"

The weak, good-looking face wreathed into a saturnine smile. "I knew it, Will. I also knew you were alive."

"You did, did you? Where'd you pick that up?"

"Jerem Burch's daughter, Ellie. I talked to her a couple of weeks ago. Maybe not even that long. She told me."

"And?" Will asked, rising and flipping a coin on the counter. "What of it?"

The man came up, too. A head taller than Will normally, he was stooped and lean with a flabby appearance. He shrugged. "I was going out to Arizona. Ellie said she was going out there."

Will nodded. "She did. She and Annalee, both. They went to Havasu."

The man rocked back on his heels. His smile wasn't unpleasant, just cynical-looking and oily. "Havasu. Hell, it sounds like a new drink. Ellie told me you got to be quite a bounty hunter out there." The fixed, smiling eyes were almost like a woman's. "I told her you had what it took to be a good one, all right."

"And what's that?" Will asked softly.

"Oh, guts. A kind of hardness. The sort that keeps a woman tied down. Full of moral responsibility and all that stuff."

Will got the innuendo all right. It made his face go shades paler. The veiled way he referred to Beth and her life with Will made the anger come out in him slowly, laced over with contempt for the kind of man who had made the remark. With hardly any conscious effort, he lifted his right arm, open handed, and swung it. The blow wasn't hard, but it spun Beacon backwards until he went over into a heap when his knees collided with the counter bench. The wide, moist eyes were glaring at the manhunter.

But Will was walking away, toward the doorway. He had never liked Beacon. The man was going to hell in his own way, and nothing would stop him until he arrived there. The talk of Beacon's remarks to married women was more than rumor, he knew. Beacon's kind weren't rare on the frontier— or anywhere—but they were pretty generally despised by real men everywhere.

For that reason Will didn't look back. Contempt forbade it. He was almost through the door when the explosion sounded, and his left leg went violently forward, throwing him off balance and sending him sprawling in the hard dirt outside the café. Shouts and curses erupted from inside. He knew what had happened even before the lashing pain tele-graphed the message of injury to his brain.

Beacon had a Derringer. He had shot Will in the leg. Twisting clear of the opening, Will swept back his coat and drew his .45 in one smooth, much practiced movement that was like fluid running downhill.

There was the sound of someone reviling Beacon from in-side. Will raised his head a little and risked an angry look in their direction. His cocked pistol was a foot ahead of his face, but he couldn't fire.

The brawny stage station hostler with his shirt tail hanging out in back was hauling Beacon to his feet with one fist and cocking the other. Will stood up, locked his teeth against the pain in his leg, and stepped through the door.

"Let him go and get out of the way!"

The hostler looked over his shoulder. There was a nasty little big-bored .41 caliber under-and-over belly gun lying be-hind his big boots. The man's indignation was evident when he spoke, indignation and scorn both. He had seen the cow-ardly shot.

"No need for that on the likes of him, mister," the hostler

said, then he fired the scarred fist. Beacon's head went back and crashed against the counter with a sickening, dull, crunching sound.

The hostler stepped back, surveyed his handiwork, and spat, then he turned to Will with the fury still in his eyes, but abating a little. "I'm sorry, pardner, but there's no call for killin' a skunk like him. I seen the whole thing. I don't know why you slapped him, but he had no call to try and shoot you in the back."

Will limped forward, holstered his gun, and saw the sea of frightened, startled faces in the room. He glanced disinterestedly at Beacon, saw the blood dripping from the man's shattered mouth, and sat down on the bench and looked at the wound through the tear in his trousers.

The hostler came over, a thick-set man, not very tall but built like a young bull. He scowled at the wound, pursed his coarse lips, and made a dry, whistling sound.

"B'Gawd, you was lucky, mister. Just nicked the outside meat is all. No broke bones. You sure was lucky." The man turned and glanced again at Beacon, unconscious and unattended where he lay. "That feller hadn't ought to even carry a gun . . . missing your back at *that* distance."

Will probed the ragged tear in his flesh and felt more relief than the hostler did, then he looked up with a small smile. "Well, I got to buy another pair of pants now."

The hostler appreciated the dry humor and grinned widely, showing teeth stained by long use of chewing tobacco. "Just sit there a spell and rig up a bandage for the thing. It'll quit bleedin' after a bit. I'll go 'round and get old man Sims to open the company store and sell you some britches. What size you take?"

Will watched the man depart and looked up in time to see the only two women in the place—the officers' wives who had gotten on at Westport — walking swiftly out of the café, heads high. He grinned, held off removing his trousers until they were gone, then peeled them off. A man in an apron of flour sacking handed him some bulky bandaging material. Will thanked the man, made a usable patchwork job of staunching the flow of blood, and bandaged the four-inch-long rip in his flesh and donned the pants the hostler brought back, paying as he transferred his wallet from the ruined pair to the new ones.

He tried walking, found it not difficult beyond a little nagging pain, and started for the door. The hostler glanced after him, over at Beacon, then called out to him.

"What you want us to do to this carrion?"

Will turned, saw the sullen, purple wreckage of Beacon's face, and smiled coldly. "He's had enough. When he comes around put him on a stage and let him go."

"All right," the hostler said doubtfully. "But, we *could* string him up. Bushwhackers get that around here, y'know."

"Yeah, I know. Don't dirty your hands." Will saw the man's nod of agreement and returned it, then limped over to the stage, smiled up at the guard and driver who were watching him sober-faced, and swung in through the door and eased down gingerly across from the two officers' wives.

Indian Wells fell behind them. Will made a cigarette and smoked it thoughtfully, conscious of the covert looks from the two women, which irritated him, and heard their muted, garbled conversation, guessed closely enough what it was about—Will Brennan and the raw frontier—and ground out the stub, seeing the dark shapes of land and brush, trees and cacti, racing rearward. An hour or so later he stuffed his wallet inside his shirt, next to his skin, tilted his hat forward, and went to sleep.

★ ★ ★ ★ ★

Dawn brought him awake with a feverish throbbing in the wounded leg. He winced from putting his weight on the thing when he changed stages, in the eerie, unwholesome light of dawn at a place he hardly remembered named Dunnigan's Crossing. The officers' wives were more than solicitous; they were lugubrious and told of his shooting at Indian Wells to anyone lazy enough to listen, including an elderly, portly man who joined them on the last lap of the trip to Cottonwood and who turned out to be an apothecary.

The apothecary was interested in an abstract, professional way. He told Will of the many gunshot wounds he'd tended to in his long years in the trade.

"Is it pretty painful?"

Will looked at the man eloquently before he answered. "I've felt better," he said dryly.

That drew an understanding smile. "I know, of course. What I meant, does it feel like a fever, locally, in the leg, or an illness in the body . . . all over, in other words?"

Will knew the man's intentions were good, but it was hard to answer without a twinge of sarcasm, too. He fished around for his tobacco sack, twisted up a cigarette, lit it, and inhaled before he spoke.

"Right now, I'd say it's pretty much all over."

"That's not very good. Infection spreads quickly." The apothecary loosened the bottom two buttons of his waistcoat with a practiced hand and let his girth expand. "If it was just the leg, I'd say the wound was feverish. Aside from gangrene, you'd be sure to recover." He drew his eyebrows inward a little before he went on. "But if you ache all over, well, then, it's a mortal cinch you've gone and taken an infection from the thing."

"Thanks," Will said shortly, smoking as though he felt

perfectly normal and ignoring the stranger.

"Look, here, suppose you let me lance the thing? I don't like to suggest it, but on the other hand I know enough about these things to know also that if it's left unattended you stand an excellent chance of dying."

Will regarded the tip of the cigarette coolly. He thought how completely ridiculous it would be to die from the bullet of a belly gun, fired at his back by a typical tinhorn coward after facing a far more likely and expected—even admirable death—under the guns of really desperate and dangerous gunmen like the Verde River Kid, and others. It struck him as so improbable and asinine that he could die like this, that he looked around at the apothecary. But the man's worried frown changed his mind in an instant.

"All right. It'll be hard to do, though, in here, won't it, without more light?"

The pill-roller shook his head. "I could tell you of far more peculiar circumstances I've done more serious jobs under." He turned and saw the two older women watching them. "Ladies, with your permission. It's necessary that I lance this leg wound. Would you oblige us both by turning your heads."

Will smiled in spite of the dullness and fever that was racking him.

The apothecary drew out a small, golden-handled penknife, seared the end of the blade with a spluttering sulphur match, and went to work.

Will felt the morning air on his legs and watched the deft, able fingers that pried away the stiffened bandage and began making neat incisions through the crusted-over accumulation of bandage fuzz over the bullet slash.

There was pain, but in small, stabbing flashes so that he had no trouble in fighting back the urge to wince away from the knife blade, then it was all over. The wound bled anew, running dark scarlet over his leg and dripping onto the floor of the old coach.

The apothecary was hunched over with a look of concentration so intense that Will held his silence until the man began to rearrange the dressing with sad shakes of his head at having to use the same, stiff cloth over again.

By the time they were conscious of the teams' slackening pace before some way station or town, Will had redressed and, uniquely enough, began to feel better almost instantly. He grinned ruefully to himself. It couldn't be that recovery could be so rapid. It must be that he believed strongly enough in what the stranger had told him, but the fact remained that he did feel a considerable abatement of the sickness, the fever, and the ache that had previously filled his tired body.

The apothecary was more than interested, too, when Will commented on his relieved feeling. "Sometimes it's like that. Not often, but sometimes. I'm so glad, too, my boy. No sense in dying if it can be helped."

"No," Will said agreeably. "Especially when you've a job that's only half done."

The apothecary looked over at the two women, saw the greenish tints to their faces, and smiled.

"No, naturally not."

In such condition and frame of mind Will came to Cottonwood, with the early afternoon rays of the sun breaking over the little town, familiar and yet strange to him, and feeling much better in mind and spirit than he had when he had left Indian Wells.

VIII

In Cottonwood, the first fresh breeze of an early fall was comb-
ing the dust out of the treetops when Will rolled in and got down
gingerly, weakly, from the coach. The nightmare ride from Indian Wells and Beacon's sneak shot was over. The ill effects lingered in the throbbing leg and the sense of physical weakness,
but otherwise he felt nothing more than great thirst and hunger
—and anxiety about Annalee that he couldn't shake and which
had been growing with the miles.

He threaded his way out of the mob clustered at the livery
barn, saw the two officers' wives pointing him out to another
elderly woman, got away from the confused bedlam, and
limped toward a saloon. He had a drink of ale, tepid and stale,
made a face at the oily taste of the stuff, and got out of the
place, looking for a café. He remembered one from years
back, but it was gone. Surprised, he studied Cottonwood objectively and slowly. The town had grown, was growing.
There was even a little park where some rather unhealthy-looking cottonwood striplings, transplanted with
more civic enthusiasm than savvy, drooped disconsolately in
the midst of the calculated, severe correctness. He smiled to
himself. Cottonwood, finally, was coming of age. It showed
the typical straight-laced and unimaginative grooming that
eventually swept over all the old hell-roaring cow towns of the
frontier that survived their infancy.

In a way it pleased him. He struck out looking for another
café, conscious that he was a stranger to most of this new Cot-

tonwood anyway. Memories came up, here and there, to bother him, but not nearly as many as he had feared might. There was even a hotel now, with a dining room. He ate, got a room, cleaned up, and stood looking at himself for a moment in the real glass mirror. He was tired all right, and drawn-looking from the siege with the wound in his leg. But he was excited, too. Wisely, though, he lay down on the lumpy bed and slept, and the darkness came up and engulfed him almost instantly. It was many hours later that he awakened, ravenous and thirsty again. Taking a bath was an awkward affair, with the sore leg, but he took one anyway, changed the bandage, made it smaller, and was glad to see the ragged flesh healing over, then he descended to the dining room and ate his fill again. When he stepped out on to the plank walk, it was with the feeling of a revitalized man. True, a limp was there, but hardly noticeable. The town was alive with early evening strollers. Strangers. He didn't recognize a single face in spite of an effort to do so. Of course, there would still be many that he knew, but they would be a minority now.

Walking proved almost a pleasure. There was the great uncertainty ahead at his destination to bother him, but the evening, the facts, the interest in this town he hadn't known in close to five years, all conspired to make him feel less the stranger than he had felt the night he had returned, not too long before, and had left within the hour of his homecoming.

The Burch house looked almost like a Christmas tree for lights, when Will came out of town toward it. He had a premonition that made his steps lose some of their buoyancy. He reinforced his lagging spirit with labored hope, and went forward, turned in at the little gate, and stalked up the walk to the porch and stood, frightened for some inexplicable reason, between two carriage lamps that burned brightly, throwing shadows across his lean face, stripped of surplus flesh and rock-hard, bronzed and flinty-looking, but not altogether detracting from his brooding handsomeness. He raised a fist and knocked.

Jerem Burch squinted up at him. "Good evening, young man. Won't you come in?"

Will shook his head. He tried to mold a smile with his features, but it was a failure. Burch's face was seamed where he didn't remember it being that way before. "No thanks. Could you ask Annalee to step to the door for a moment?"

"Annalee?" Burch said doubtfully. "Well, I'm sure you'll understand, young man. You see . . . she's with a group of friends right now. They're having a party."

"Oh," Will said uncertainly. "I'm sorry. I didn't know. Well . . . just for a moment, perhaps?"

"I'll see," Burch said. "It's an engagement party. She and young Stallings. He's the stage line representative here in Cottonwood. You know him, no doubt."

Will was hard hit. He stood like a tree fighting against the mighty power of a windstorm, erect, forbidding, and badly shaken. "No doubt," he echoed hollowly. He let one picture come down into his mind. The startled look on the stage line clerk's face when he asked where a good place was to go in Arizona. The hopes were dying inside of him somewhere, buried under tons of anguish and shock.

Burch was still squinting into the lean, mahogany features with their impassiveness. There was something vaguely familiar about the young man. He shook his head finally, irritably, in resignation. "I'm sorry young man, but . . . dammit . . . I just can't seem to call your name to mind."

Will shrugged. He knew how dead his face was beginning to look now. This was the final sifting of bitter ashes over the grave of his hopes.

"It won't make much difference, but . . . well . . . would you ask Annalee to tell you the name of Beth Brennan's baby, and bring it back to me here at the door?"

Burch's face showed his surprise at the unique request, but he nodded without speaking and turned away, leaving the door wide open.

Will could hear the sound of voices. They seemed to reflect a carefree happiness he had never heard at a party before. Of course, his knowledge of parties was extremely limited, too. When he and Beth had married, it had been a simple, one-dollar ceremony. There had been no parties in his earlier years, either.

He heard the wonderful lightheartedness diminish suddenly and surmised Jerem Burch was talking to Annalee. It was all like something happening a long way off, strained through the shock that was slowly, so slowly, wearing off. But the sounds didn't revive. He stood still, shadowed in the wavering light, a lean, broad-shouldered man with unpleasant blue eyes in a set, stony face that had a handsome mouth full of fading tolerance and nearly forgotten humor.

It was like that when Annalee saw him. She came uncertainly, slowly, into the empty hallway, looking up with great black eyes in a cameo-like face toward the silent stranger in the doorway, back a foot or two. They stood looking at one another, saying nothing. Annalee walked closer and the color came back with a rush.

"Will!"

"Annalee. I had to know the baby's name. Beth's baby. I got it over at Thistleton. Ball's dead. Lynched over there."

"It *was* Beth, then, Will?"

He nodded. "Yes. They're both buried there. Side by side. I . . . have the baby, only . . . I don't know her name."

"Her name's Carey, Will."

Annalee had both hands locked together in front of her. She walked closer to him, stood looking up into his face, searching his features, seeing the pain moving in the background of his eyes. Her hands parted, reaching out to him.

He stared at her thinking how beautiful she was. A woman now. The girl he had always considered her was as dead as— his wife. An ironic thought offered the suggestion that what she had been through since she had known him—since he had come back—was enough to make a woman out of any girl, enough certainly to dissolve the girl Annalee had been.

He inclined his head gallantly. "Then I'm going to change her name a little. I'll call her Careylee."

Annalee didn't thrust herself at him. She moved softly, slowly. "Will . . . please . . . take a walk with me."

He looked over her head a little, saw the curious eyes of several people looking at them. "You . . . have guests, Annalee."

"No, it doesn't matter. It can't matter, Will. It has to be *now*." She moved past him a little, hesitated, and looked up. "Please?" He nodded again, turned, and went along behind her.

Annalee didn't turn toward the plank walk that would take them up toward town. Instead, she swung to her left and went around the house. Will followed in the darkness of a moonless night, and the little dog next door began to bark excitedly. It was as dark as the inside of a well in the tree-shaded backyard.

They stopped, and Will slitted his eyes to make out old remembered landmarks. The dog's noise subsided into garrulous little snufflings, and the massive chorus of crickets took over the darkness again.

"Annalee?"

"Yes? I'm here. Can't you see me?"

177

"No, I can't even see my own hand."

He felt her small, warm fingers go inside his hand and around it. He stood perfectly still then, content for eternity to roll on, allowing him to stand exactly as he was, with that small, soft hand in his.

"Come on. I . . . just didn't want to take you over *there*. But I'll have to. I had no idea it was so dark out. We had a candle burning out . . . here . . . tonight. The grape arbor."

Will felt her twist and look up at him. He couldn't see anything but a small, perfect oval, in the gloom, and, when she gave a small tug, he went along readily enough and ducked his head as they went in among the vines. There was a bitter-sweet smell in the arbor, a foreign scent to the man from burned and blasted rangelands of the distant areas where his sorrow had driven him. He liked it, somehow.

The light was a frail thing, showing little more than outlines, concealing flatness and highlighting the prominent planes of faces and figures. Annalee let go of his hand and faced him.

"Will? Did you see Ellie before you left Havasu?"

He nodded somberly. "Yes." That was all he said. The memory of that stormy parting was like blasphemy, in the arbor. He didn't want to discuss it.

"Well, didn't she say anything?"

He glanced wryly down into her face. "Yes, she did, but I didn't stay to hear it all."

"But, Will, you're engaged to her."

He started violently, staring down at the beautiful features with their wonderfully parted lips over small, even teeth. "I am?" he said. "Annalee! The devil I am!"

"But she told me you were. Said so the morning you rode out after those men. After Ball and those others, you remember? After you left, she came in and . . . well . . . we talked."

178

"After I kissed you," he said brutally.

"All right, after we kissed and you rode away. Anyway, she came in and told me you and she were engaged."

"Annalee, listen to me. I'm all kinds of a fool. I'll go no further." Will was amazed the way the right words seemed to come so readily to him. "You said once that you knew a whale of a lot more than I thought you did. Well, all right. What do you know about me?"

Her answer was just as spontaneous as his question. Each was surprised and neither suspected that they were reaching for a straw that was slipping away from them.

"I know that you're killing yourself. You're racing against time . . . and all the men who want to kill you. You're trying to beat yourself down, wear yourself out, before a bullet kills you. You. . . ."

"No. I don't mean like that. I mean about me personally. What do you know?" He stopped, looking at her and shaking his head. "No, let me change that. What do you *think* of me?"

Annalee's mouth was quivering. She was fighting to control the sobs that were building up inside of her, but she couldn't hide the shine of tears in her eyes, so she gave him stare for stare, almost defiantly, when she spoke.

"I'll tell you that, too, Will Brennan. I'll be glad to. Dog-goned glad to, in fact." Her voice caught then, and she didn't speak for a long moment. The raveling of the candle was flickering under the gentleness of a tiny, stray waft of fragrant night air.

"Annalee!" The call startled them both. Will's head came up quickly with a challengingly little flaring of the nostrils. Jerem Burch was standing in the entrance to the arbor, a lighted lantern held out high, near his head. Surprise and annoyance showed in the banker's eyes. "Did I hear you raise your voice?"

Annalee turned a little, just her head, and looked at her father. There was anger showing in the way she stood, too. There was just one brusque nod, then her answer. "Yes, you did. I told Will I'll be dog-goned glad to tell him what I think of him. Maybe you'd like to stay and hear it, too?"

Burch moved closer, read the tenseness in their faces, and looked bewildered by it. "Now, child . . . what about your guests? What about young Stallings? After all. . . ."

"After all," Annalee fired right back, "I'm engaged to him, aren't I? All right, I was an idiot for a moment, let my guard down once and find myself engaged to a man I don't love . . . never can love and never will love! Does that answer your questions about him?"

Her hands were clenched together now. It was taking every ounce of her restraint to hold back the hysteria that came whirling out of nowhere, gyrating in growing circles inside her head, threatening to erupt any moment.

"And the guests . . . what about them? There are things done, honey," Burch said quietly, visibly shaken by his daughter's wild denunciation and striving to help her without knowing how, or what had caused her outburst. "They must not be allowed to slip away . . . they cannot be recaptured."

Will was shaken, too, but he saw the condition of the slip of a girl and interrupted curtly to head off the certain climax, forgetting his own inner turmoil. "Sir, will you leave us for a moment? I'll bring her back to the house shortly."

Jerem Burch looked into Will's face, read the pain there, opened his mouth to speak when Annalee swung fully toward him. The bitterness she was controlling came seeping out like acid. "Pa, you raised one daughter you've always known was no good. Please . . . let the other daughter try, just once more, to get out of the shadow of the reputation Ellie has always managed to stigmatize me with, will you? Just once!"

Burch was out of his element and floundering. He lowered the lantern because his arm ached from holding it aloft, more than because of the confusion he felt.

"All right, Annalee . . . honey. But please . . . the guests. . . ."

He walked back the way he had come. Annalee and Will watched the lantern bobbing around the side of the house. When it was gone, Annalee turned back. A lot of the fire was gone from her eyes, but the shine of near tears was still there.

"All right, Will Brennan, here's what I think of you. You let Beth's husband go. You didn't have to . . . probably shouldn't have . . . but you let him go. Whether he had a lynching coming or not, I don't know, but I *do* know that, if you had been beside him, you'd have died fighting a mob." She bit her lip, watching the tawny, pale look in his face. "And . . . Carey. You. . . ."

"Careylee," he interrupted stiffly.

"Careylee, then. You didn't have to bring her back or even go after her. You didn't have to strap yourself with her. She's not yours, Will Brennan."

"Oh, yes, she is. She's mine, Annalee, and she'll *be* mine until the day she marries. Don't ever forget it, either!"

"That's what I mean." Annalee was calming down now. The wrath was ashes, but the embers still showed in her face, and they were being put out by two small tears, one from each eye, that limped painfully, slowly, down the full roundness of her tan-gold cheeks. "That's what I mean, Will." She looked away from him for the second time since they had come to the grape arbor. "You're well . . . noble. Ellie lied. I suspected it, too."

"Then why," he said dryly, "did you leave?"

"I wanted *you* to make the decision between us. That's why I came home. To wait."

Will thought how girlish her profile was, but it didn't show in the quiet, wry way he spoke. "You didn't wait long, Annalee."

She motioned curtly toward the house. "Will, you didn't come. I went down to see each stage come in. The days went by. Stallings . . . well . . . that's how it happened. He thought I walked down there to see him. But he's nice, Will. Anyway, the days went by. You should've been here before. . . ."

"I couldn't have gotten here any sooner. I had to go to Thistleton to get the baby . . . to get Careylee. There was this other thing, too, Annalee. You knew about that. I wasn't sure who she was or anything else. I had to go over there and find out. You, yourself, wanted to know if it was Beth."

Annalee didn't answer right away. She sniffed slightly first. "Well, now that you're here . . . what?"

Will reached out and touched her. He could feel the limpness turn to something stiff, like dread, and didn't pull her in close. "Well?" he said softly.

She shook her head at him. "No. Not that way. It isn't even yours."

"It *is* mine, Annalee. Sure, Careylee's got to have a mother, but I can hire one of those, I reckon. But that's not it. Listen, that's why I asked you if you knew such a whale of a lot. Just to show you how much you don't know and haven't even come close to guessing . . . did you know that I'm in love with you? Did you know I despise your sister? Did you know that I used to go to the storeroom of the Federal Eagle, in Havasu, and get dead drunk so I could blot out the memory of a woman's face? The woman who had usurped Beth's place? Annalee, I could keep you here all night telling you things you couldn't have guessed, but, really, there's only one thing I'd hoped you *had* guessed. That I love you. That I want you as my wife. And I came back to Cottonwood for that one purpose . . . to ask you to marry me. I loved you long before I found Careylee, too. I came back to tell you all these things . . . and walk in on your engagement party."

Annalee couldn't make a sound. The agony of tears finally overwhelmed her defenses and shook her. Will took her in close and held her tightly until most of the anguish had subsided, then he reached under her chin and tilted back the flushed, tear-stained face.

"Annalee, will you marry me?"

She had thought he would kiss her, but when he didn't, she smiled wistfully up at him. "Yes. I've wanted to say that, or just something close to it for . . . oh, Will, if you'd just held out a hand, beckoned to me, or even nodded and smiled, I'd have come to you. I've waited so dog-goned long, Will. Darn it! I'm not a mule. I've got feelings, too. But Will, I *do* love you, and have loved you for so long, but . . . I'd just about given up."

He understood the incoherence of the swift half sentences when his head went down. The kiss was gentle and reverent. If a wee tincture of Burch passion entered into it, there was ample and good reason, and Will's blood responded. It was the kind of mating that was predestined in eons gone when the clay of ancestors conspired to create the perfect match and sustained its possibility through centuries of building the lineages that would make such a pair inviolable for all time, united as one in a supreme union.

Will let Annalee's mouth free itself, but he held her still closer, marveling at the pristine clearness of the night now that his eyes were accustomed to its shades of purple and, also, now that his troubled spirit and tortured mine were free again. He dredged up a little prayer from his boyhood. It wasn't exactly appropriate, being a table grace, but it was thanks, and he said it to himself, then he pushed her at arm's length.

"Darling, Stallings . . . what about him?" The uneasiness was returning again. "It isn't right to . . . well . . . he's got feelings."

"It would be something like that, wouldn't it?" She didn't give him a chance to inquire into the remark. One hand took a lacy handkerchief from her bosom and used it to touch the ravages passion had brought on her face. "Let me do it, Will. You . . . wait here."

He winced. "Not now. Not at your party. My Lord, Annalee . . . !"

"Will . . . darling, it won't be any easier tomorrow. Just wait here. Don't move . . . will you?"

He kissed her again and shook his head. "No, ma'am. You couldn't get me out of this arbor with a span of oxen."

She left him alone, threading her way back toward the house, and the night closed in with its heavy scent of grapes and the incessant noise of crickets.

And he was still sitting there under the arbor when the party broke up and the guests left. He heard them laughing and talking around in front and wondered how Stallings felt. It made him uncomfortable, yet he marveled at Annalee for being able to salvage the remnants of the party's lag and conclude it successfully. He had no idea how long he had been there in the coolness of the arbor with the night for a friend.

It wasn't until he heard his name called and looked up to see Jerem Burch coming in among the vines that he straightened on the bench and forced his mind back to the present.

"Will Brennan! By golly, lad, no wonder I didn't recognize you. It's been years, boy, years. Of course, I heard some of this talk that you weren't dead, but just lately."

Will moved his hat, watching the older man seating himself. There was an offered cigar case. Burch accepted the bounty hunter's refusal in good grace and lighted his own.

The night was still and cool around them, waiting. Will sat in uncomfortable expectancy, then Burch spoke.

"I don't know exactly what to say."

"Annalee told you . . . sir?"

A slow nod. "Yes."

Will's discomfort made him squirm on the bench. "Did she . . . has she . . . told young Stallings, too?"

He got another nod.

"How did he take it?"

"Better than I would have, I promise you." The cigar smoke seemed to foul the other, less sturdy odors in the arbor. "He's a fine boy, Will. A little young, perhaps, but a good boy. I always have liked him."

Will slumped forward a little. "He probably took it better than I would have, too," he said dryly. "Especially since it was Annalee."

Jerem Burch's composure seemed to desert him a little at a time. He had carried a great load for a long time and was about to relinquish it, or make an effort to.

"Will, you and Annalee . . . well . . . it seems like this thing was inevitable. I'm surprised, of course, but calmer reflection doesn't indicate any cause for alarm . . . in me . . . as her father. I won't say I'm happy about the Stallings business, nor over the tongue wagging that's bound to crop up now, but I'm sure neither of you is childish enough to be making a mistake. This has been awfully sudden . . . abrupt, sort of. Like an avalanche." He shot a glance at Will. "Don't get me wrong, Will. It's not that I disapprove of you at all. It's just . . . the suddenness of it. You understand, don't you?"

Will nodded slowly without looking up from an inspection of the ground underfoot. "Yes, I think so. Especially the way it happened. At her engagement party to young Stallings. I understand your side of it, I think."

Burch looked at him pensively. What he saw was a young man whose sadness and experiences had made him grave, mature, and old-seeming. It awed the banker just a little and confirmed a thought he had.

"Will, there's something else. I don't know exactly if you're the man for it, but I feel that you are." Will turned, saw the indecision and something akin to pain in Jerem Burch's face. He said nothing, waiting.

"It's Ellie. Lord, Will, it's hard for a father to understand it. A widower's the saddest kind of a father."

Will's mind went instantly to the blacksmith over at Thistleton. He recalled the man's boundless compassion with a sudden comprehension, a poignant appreciation.

"What is it you want me to do?"

Burch firmed up his resolve and put the thought into blunt words that cost him a lot. "Get her to stay . . . away from Cottonwood." He turned instantly to the younger man. "That's a terrible thing for a father to say. I know what you're thinking. As God is my witness, Will, I've tried everything. Prayer . . . everything."

Will shook his head, not looking at Burch, offering to let the older man salvage his dignity. "No, I partly understand, Mister Burch." He paused, then went on. "I thought a lot about Ellie on my way here from Havasu. Had reason to, after a stop at a place called Indian Wells. It isn't cruel to say what you've just put into words. It takes guts, and I know it does. You see, I'm no relation to her at all . . . not even a friend . . . and I thought along the same lines."

"You'll do it, then, Will? Persuade her to stay away from Cottonwood? It's her sister's happiness I'm thinking of now. In the house, just now, earlier . . . Annalee told me lots of things . . . after she left you out here tonight."

Will was startled. "Mister Burch, Annalee's happiness is

in no danger from Ellie as far as *I'm* concerned. Not now or ever. I can promise you that."

"It isn't just that, Will," Burch said, "that was a consideration with me, naturally, but I hardly had any qualms there."

Will made a cigarette. "You don't have much to worry about, anyway." He debated a long time before he decided to say this. "I talked to Ellie before I came back. It wasn't pleasant, either. Then, at Indian Wells where the stage stopped to change horses, I met Beacon. You remember him?" Burch nodded slowly, painfully, averting his head so the bitterness wouldn't show. Will looked away, too, from the slump in the older man's shoulders. This wasn't pleasant to say, or listen to, but it was the truth and needed airing, here and now. The situation had solved itself in the usual way of natural solutions, with a simple, effective, and bittersweet ending.

"Well, Beacon was heading into Arizona . . . to Havasu, I reckon." He smoked for a moment. The shooting wasn't relevant here, or necessary to relate. It didn't bear on Ellie, except very indirectly, anyway. "If they stay there, it won't be for long. They're the kind that'll have to keep moving, always, until . . . well. . . ."

"Yes," the older man said quietly, "I understand. Until Ellie comes to her senses. Gets burned out, old, maybe. Then she'll come home." He looked up at Will. "There'll *be* a home for her then, too . . . won't there, Will?"

"Sure there will. All three of us'll ke_p it for her, Mister Burch."

Burch stood up. The lantern he'd brought into the arbor with him was flickering from an untended wick. "Annalee's coming. I'll go. This was all . . . between us?"

"Yes, sir," Will said, arising.

He watched the banker go back toward the house, making his way through the dense foliage of shrubbery toward the back door, avoiding his daughter.

Annalee came into the arbor, looking up into his face and seeing the soberness of it. Her eyes were questioning. "Is there anything wrong, Will?"

It struck him as being ironically humorless. He smiled a trifle. "I don't think so, dear. Just a million little things, all tied together. Annalee . . . darling, will you marry me before I go back to Havasu?"

"Go back?" She grew rigid, staring at him. "I thought we'd live at your ranch. Fix it up and live out there. Oh, darling! We belong in Cottonwood . . . not Havasu."

He went over and put his arms around her, smiling. "Sure, we'll fix up the ranch and live in Cottonwood. I didn't mean I was going back to stay, but I've got to go over there and get Careylee. I've got to thank Clem and the Dexters and pay Maude, some way, for all she's done."

Annalee put her head over on to his shoulder, pushing against him, then she pulled it back quickly and glanced up at him again. "Will Brennan, you asked me to marry you. By golly, you're not going to get out of it, either."

He laughed at her. "I have no desire to, honey. It's just that I've got to. . . ."

"You never mind all that. First, we'll be married, then *I'll* go to Havasu and get our baby, and then. . . ."

"But, honey, you can't travel alone. It . . . just isn't done."

"Don't fret about that. I'll take a girl friend with me, but I'm going, not you."

"Well," Will said, looking over her shoulder with a wry grin. "Just what am I supposed to do while you're away?"

Annalee saw victory ahead. A lot of the stiffness went out of her. It wasn't altogether the fact that Ellie would be in Havasu, waiting, she felt certain, to see Will again; it was also the little ties he'd created unconsciously in the desert-fringe town that might delay him. She had no intention of letting either remind him of past unhappiness. He'd had more than one man's share of grief in the hectic few months since he'd come back from the Army. She fully intended to shield him as much as possible, now and in the future, from new hurts.

"That's easy." Annalee stepped back and cocked her head to one side. "You can go out to the ranch and start fixing things up." She was watching him closely. Instinctively she knew he would have to face all the old ghosts of his unhappy past alone.

"No, on second thought, you hire some carpenters and . . . whatever . . . and send them out, then, when I get back we'll both go out and supervise things." She knew it would torture the other way. If she was to help him find himself again, this would be her first battle, and with him, too, not others. "How does that sound to you?"

He smiled. "Have I any choice, ma'am? Aren't you pretty well laying down the law?"

But she saw the relief in his face, too, and made a stab at humor herself. "Nights, you can cook for Pa. He can't fry an egg."

Will's grin faded before the startled glance he shot at her. "No, listen, Annalee . . . my gosh . . . your dad and I'd both be dead from ptomaine poisoning before you got back. I'm not even a good camp cook."

"Well, then," she promised, inwardly relieved at the quick victory over their fixing up his deserted ranch, "you two can eat out. It won't be for long anyway. I ought to be back within four or five days."

"Oh, we'll manage. I'll shop around and hire a girl to come in and do the cooking."

"No, you won't! You and Pa can eat out. It'll do both of you good to get out evenings . . . together."

Then he did laugh. Throwing his head back and letting the sound burst out of the grape arbor, boom into the still darkness around them, and taper off until the sound was taken up by the little dog next door that barked aimlessly but excitedly when his slumbers were interrupted.

"Well," Annalee said with a wry grin and a single shake of her head. "I haven't finally found you, Will Brennan, to lose you to some woman who can cook better than I can. Besides, seriously, I like the idea of you and Pa going out together of an evening. It'll . . . well . . . it'll help stop the gossip that's bound to come up now."

"I reckon," he said, still smiling and finding it very hard to look sober again. "Gossip never lasts long, though, not in a town that's growing as fast as Cottonwood is."

"Will? Do you like two-handed poker?"

He nodded, a little puzzled by the irrelevancy of it.

"Good. That's Pa's weakness." She went up close to him. "Darling, it won't be for long . . . and . . . I love you so much, Will Brennan, so very, very much. Tell me you love me again."

He did.

LAURAN PAINE

THE KILLER GUN

It is no ordinary gun. It is specially designed to help its owner kill a man. George Mars has customized a Colt revolver so it will fire when it is on half cock, saving the time it takes to pull back the hammer before firing. But then the gun is stolen from Mars's shop. Mars has engraved his name on it but, as the weapon passes from hand to hand, owner to owner, killer to killer, his identity becomes as much of a mystery as why possession of the gun skews the odds in any duel. And the legend of the killer gun grows with each newly slain man.

___4875-2 $4.50 US/$5.50 CAN